# "Do You Propose Marriage To Every Woman You Have Sex With?"

He stared at her as though she'd slapped him.

"What kind of question is that?"

"One you might want to take a look at. You say you can't control your reactions to me and this is your way of having sex without guilt. Well, thank you for the offer," she said, her heart crumbling into aching pieces. "But I believe I'll pass."

He looked shocked. Guess he'd never been turned down before. She fought the tears that threatened. The last thing she wanted was for him to know how devastated she was by his reasons for proposing. The irony didn't escape her. Her youth had been filled with dreams of the time when he'd propose to her.

And now that he had, she'd refused him....

Dear Reader,

Welcome to another fabulous month at Silhouette Desire, where we offer you the best in passionate, powerful and provocative love stories. You'll want to delve right in to our latest DYNASTIES: THE DANFORTHS title with Anne Marie Winston's highly dramatic *The Enemy's Daughter*— you'll never guess who the latest Danforth bachelor has gotten involved with! And the steam continues to rise when Annette Broadrick returns to the Desire line with a brand-new series, THE CRENSHAWS OF TEXAS. These four handsome brothers will leave you breathless, right from the first title, *Branded*.

Read a Silhouette Desire novel from *his* point of view in our new promotion MANTALK. Eileen Wilks continues this series with her highly innovative and intensely emotional story *Meeting at Midnight*. Kristi Gold continues her series THE ROYAL WAGER with another confirmed bachelor about to meet his match in *Unmasking the Maverick Prince*. How comfortable can *A Bed of Sand* be? Well, honey, if you're lying on it with the hero of Laura Wright's latest novel…who cares! And the always enjoyable Roxanne St. Claire, whom *Publishers Weekly* calls "an author who's on the fast track to making her name a household one," is scorching up the pages with *The Fire Still Burns*.

Happy reading,

*Melissa Jeglinski*

Melissa Jeglinski
Senior Editor, Silhouette Desire

Please address questions and book requests to:
Silhouette Reader Service
U.S.: 3010 Walden Ave., P.O. Box 1325, Buffalo, NY 14269
Canadian: P.O. Box 609, Fort Erie, Ont. L2A 5X3

# ANNETTE BROADRICK

## BRANDED

Silhouette®

*Desire*

Published by Silhouette Books

**America's Publisher of Contemporary Romance**

SILHOUETTE BOOKS

ISBN 0-373-76604-1

BRANDED

Copyright © 2004 by Annette Broadrick

All rights reserved. Except for use in any review, the reproduction
or utilization of this work in whole or in part in any form by any
electronic, mechanical or other means, now known or hereafter
invented, including xerography, photocopying and recording, or in
any information storage or retrieval system, is forbidden without
the written permission of the editorial office, Silhouette Books,
233 Broadway, New York, NY 10279 U.S.A.

All characters in this book have no existence outside the imagination of
the author and have no relation whatsoever to anyone bearing the same
name or names. They are not even distantly inspired by any individual
known or unknown to the author, and all incidents are pure invention.

This edition published by arrangement with Harlequin Books S.A.

® and TM are trademarks of Harlequin Books S.A., used under license.
Trademarks indicated with ® are registered in the United States Patent
and Trademark Office, the Canadian Trade Marks Office and in other
countries.

Visit Silhouette Books at www.eHarlequin.com

**Printed in U.S.A.**

**Books by Annette Broadrick**

## *ANNETTE BROADRICK*

believes in romance and the magic of life. Since 1984, Annette has shared her view of life and love with readers. In addition to being nominated by *Romantic Times* magazine as one of the Best New Authors of that year, she has also won the *Romantic Times* Reviewers' Choice Award for Best in its Series, the *Romantic Times* W.I.S.H. award, and the *Romantic Times* Lifetime Achievement Awards for Series Romance and Series Romantic Fantasy.

# Prologue

The Crenshaws were having a barbecue and everyone for miles around had been invited. Strings of lights decorated the large live oaks surrounding the hacienda-style homestead and dozens of tiki lamps discouraged mosquitoes. The patio had been cleared for dancing to the music of a local country-western band. Joe finished serving the last of the line of guests barbecued ribs, beef and sausage he'd prepared, pleased to see everyone having fun. He and Gail always enjoyed giving parties.

"Fill you a plate and c'mon over here and sit down, Joe," Randy, one of his friends, called. "We've been talking about the Crenshaw family and my grandson's asking all kinds of questions I can't answer."

Joe laughed, filled his plate and ambled over to the long picnic table where he sat down with some of the guests. After polishing off some ribs, Joe asked, "What's your questions, Teddy?"

The twelve-year-old blushed. "I was wondering how long the Crenshaws have lived here."

"Since 1845."

Teddy's eyes rounded. "Wow!"

"Yep, it's been a long time since Jeremiah Crenshaw rode in to Texas. Back then, it was still a republic. So we've been here longer than Texas has been a state."

"What made him come to the Hill Country?"

"He'd heard about the area from people he'd met after he arrived in Texas. When he checked out the place, he knew this was where he wanted to settle. Luckily for him, the Republic was struggling financially and he bought the land at a good price."

"How much land?"

Before Joe could answer Teddy's question, Randy said, "It's not polite to ask how much land a person has, son. It's like asking how much money a man's got in the bank."

Joe grinned. "Oh, I don't think Jeremiah would have been offended by the question. He was proud of his holdings. I don't have the exact figures in front of me, but I know it was several thousand acres. He tended to keep track of it in miles rather than acres."

"I betcha he had to hire a bunch of people to work for him, didn't he?"

"That's true and once again J.C. lucked out. Once Texas joined the United States the following year, people from back East headed to Texas, where land was plentiful and cheap. Jeremiah sold off small parcels of land to those who wanted to work for him. He built homes and bachelor quarters for those who didn't want to buy."

"How did he feed so many people?" Teddy asked.

Joe grinned. "He was a wheeler-dealer, that's for sure. He convinced the railroad owners to run tracks out here. That way he could ship his cattle, wool and leather products out and have needed supplies shipped back."

"Was New Eden already a town?"

"More like a settlement at first. Some people didn't want to ranch, so mercantile stores and livery stables and—"

"—And saloons!"

"And saloons, as well as feed stores and a hotel, were built around the end of the railroad line. Back then, the town was called Trail's End."

Randy said, "Well, I'll be. I never knew that. You sure know your history, Joe."

"It helped that as the years passed, some of the wives of the Crenshaw men decided to keep a sort of diary of events that eventually formed a history of the family and the area. My dad had it published several years back. You could find a copy in the library, if you want to know more."

The table discussion turned to other things but Joe kept thinking about Crenshaw history. Once the others decided to listen to the live band and maybe dance some, Joe wandered over to the edge of the crowd and sat in one of the lawn chairs ranged beneath one of the large live oak trees.

The party was just one of many traditions handed down in the family. As time passed, schools and churches had been built, bringing in more people. The family helped newcomers settle and adjust to the western frontier. The common threat of Indian raids, rustlers and drought, as well as the loneliness that was part of living in Texas at the time, drew people together and forged the character of those who fought to keep their property. The Crenshaw heirs had always considered themselves guardians of their land. Each one inherited Jeremiah's strength, determination, toughness and a rowdiness that was a part of life in Texas, Joe thought, smiling.

Eventually the ranch and other holdings were incorporated, making each member of the family a shareholder as well as apportioning land to each family. Even now there was more than enough land to provide every Crenshaw with a large lot on which to build a home. Not all of them chose to work the land, but there was no question that they belonged to the Hill Country.

His second-in-command on the ranch, Kenneth Sullivan, walked over to where Joe sat, carrying a couple of long-necked bottles of beer.

"Hope you don't mind if I join you, Joe," he said.

"Not at all. Glad to have the company. I like getting away for a while to watch everyone enjoying themselves."

Ken settled into the chair next to Joe and handed him one of the beers. "They're doing that, all right, especially Ashley. I can't thank you enough for throwing this birthday party for her. Sixteen is a pretty important milestone in a girl's life."

"My four guys counted the days, remember? They could hardly wait to get their driver's license so they could drive somewhere besides on the ranch."

Ken nodded to a group gathered beneath a cluster of trees on the other side of the clearing where the party was taking place. "It's hard enough for me to get used to the idea that my Ashley's growing up so fast, but I swear those boys of yours are adding inches to their height every day!"

Joe smiled. "Not to mention the increased food bill. When Jake returned home from college a couple of years ago, there was a noticeable increase in the amount of food hauled into the house."

Ken laughed and said, "You got to admit he's putting in some long hours now that he's officially in charge of the livestock on the ranch."

"He always has, Ken. I told Gail the other night I figure he must be old Jeremiah come back in the flesh. He loves this place. I couldn't be more pleased that he's taking over for me."

He watched his tall, broad-shouldered, narrow-hipped and deeply tanned sons, their bodies honed by nature into mean, lean, fighting machines—each one too handsome for his own good.

The oldest—Jake—was twenty-four.

Jared, recently graduated from college at twenty-two, was already showing his skill at finding oil. He loved the land as well and was making plans to look for oil on the Crenshaw property.

At twenty, Jude was living up to the Crenshaw men's reputation as rowdy and reckless.

The youngest, Jason, was eighteen and still in high school. Unfortunately, he considered Jude to be the perfect role model and was well on his way to building his own reputation as a hell-raiser.

"Hi there, you two," Gail said, walking up to Joe and Ken. "The party's a success, don't you think?" she said, sounding a little breathless. She had been dancing the two-step and Joe had watched her graceful moves, thinking she looked barely old enough to vote. The band now played a slow, romantic song.

"Looks like," he agreed amiably. "You having fun?"

She laughed. "I always have fun throwing a party, as you well know. Will you come dance with me?"

"Have you ever heard me turn down the opportunity to get my arms around you?" he asked, winking at Ken. He stood and dropped his arm around her shoulder. "C'mon, Ken. It's time for you to find a dance partner."

The Crenshaw sons watched the revelry from a safe distance. None of them cared all that much for dancing and they'd made themselves scarce by standing in the shadows.

Jake had been keeping a protective eye on Ashley for most of the evening, amused and pleased to see her enjoying her party.

Ashley had been a tomboy all her life, preferring jeans and western-style shirts to frills and dresses. Seeing her tonight all dressed up had been a shock to him. The short skirt revealed shapely legs, and the combination of a special hairdo—instead of the braid she generally wore—and her carefully made-up face caused a strange and uncomfortable stirring inside him.

She was born on the ranch and had been a large part of his life since she was old enough to follow him around. She'd ridden with him on his horse by the time she was three or four years old and continued to do so until she was old enough to ride alone. He'd kept an eye on her while she tagged along with him to watch ranch hands rewire fences and haul feed when the area hadn't received enough rain to provide enough vegetation for the cattle, sheep and goats.

She'd generally had two or three dogs following her around the place, strays that had quickly found a home once they discovered her soft heart.

There was no sign of that child now. Tonight, she looked like a young woman, provocative and alluring, which bothered him for some reason.

"Looks like your little shadow has grown up, Jake."

Jake glanced at Jude with a half smile. "That she has," he replied thoughtfully.

"It's hard to believe she's sixteen," Jared said, watching Ashley dance the two-step with her dad. "I can still remember how she used to dog your footsteps when we were kids. I never understood where you got your patience."

Jake smiled. "I never minded."

"Not even when she kept telling everybody that she planned to marry you when she grew up?"

"Aw, c'mon. She was—what, six or seven years old? Kid stuff, Jared. She outgrew it."

Jason, who was two years older than Ashley, said, "I wonder if she'd go out with me now? She always laughed before whenever I asked her. Maybe I should try again now that she's older."

Jake frowned. "Considering the reputation you've worked so hard to acquire, I seriously doubt that Ken will let you anywhere near his daughter."

Jason's cheeks turned red. "C'mon, Jake. You know I wouldn't try anything with her. Ken would tear me to bits."

"And when he got through with you, I'd be waiting my turn," Jake replied.

Jude gave Jake a level look. "Why don't *you* date her?"

Jake looked at him, wondering if Jude had lost his mind. "You're kidding, right? I'm much too old for her. Besides, she's always been like a little sister to me." His eyes followed her as she changed partners. "I have to admit, though, that she doesn't look like anybody's little sister in that dress."

"Like I said, she's all grown up. So when are you going to ask her to dance?" Jude teased.

"She prizes her toes too much to want to dance with me," Jake drawled with a slow grin. "She looks to be doing just fine without me. Look at the line of guys waiting to dance with her."

"So, Jake," Jared said. "How do you feel about Dad talking retirement now that you're back home for good?"

"I think he and Mom deserve to take it a little easier," Jake replied. "Mom's already looking at house plans for a smaller place she wants to build down the road a piece. I haven't seen her this excited in a long time. She said she hopes to get Dad to do more traveling. I told 'em to go for it."

He took a drink from his beer before he said to Jared, "I'd be glad to share some of the workload with you, if you'd decide to stay in one place for longer than it takes to drill a well."

"Tending animals 24/7 isn't my idea of fun, bro. I'm happy doing what I do."

"What about you, Jude?" Jake asked. "You want to try your hand at ranching?"

"I don't mind helping out whenever you need me, Jake, you know that, but I sure don't want to make a career of it. Who knows what I'll end up doing. Right now I'm just enjoying life."

Jake's eyebrow raised. "According to Sheriff Boynton, you've been enjoying life a little too much these days. It wouldn't hurt you to work a little harder at staying out of trouble. You could take on more responsibility around here, you know."

"So Dad keeps saying," he replied defensively. "I have to listen to his lectures. I sure don't have to listen to yours."

Someone touched Jake's sleeve and he turned to find Ashley standing at his elbow, smiling at him. She wore her dark hair pulled back from her face, tumbling onto her shoulders in natural waves. Her green eyes sparkled up at him as she said, "May I talk to you, Jake?" she asked.

"Sure." He was surprised when she turned and walked away from his brothers.

She waited until they were several yards from his brothers to speak. "Dance with me," she said wistfully. "I've danced with practically everybody here…except you."

He was already shaking his head before she finished speaking. "Not me, honey. There's a bunch of guys over there mooning over you. Get one of them to dance. You don't want to dance with an old guy like me."

"Old! Twenty-four isn't old."

"It is where you're concerned," he replied without smiling.

She dropped her gaze and looked back at the party. "The party's great, isn't it?" she said, without looking at him. "Your mom and dad have been wonderful, getting this all set up."

"I'm glad you're enjoying it. The folks enjoy throwing parties and Mom had fun planning this one."

"Well, I guess I'll go back and..." Her voice trailed off. She turned back to Jake and said, "If you won't dance, at least give me a birthday kiss."

Jake nodded. He'd kissed her on her nose when she was a kid, causing her to giggle. Now that she was so grown up, he would kiss her cheek, he decided. At least, that was his plan. Only it didn't turn out that way.

She slid her arms around his neck and stood on tiptoe, pressed closely against him. He placed his hands at her waist and when he bent to kiss her, she quickly turned her head and caught his mouth with hers.

He stiffened and attempted to pull away, but she clung to him so tenaciously he didn't want to hurt her. Her soft, moist lips pressed firmly against his, her tongue playfully darting at the seam of his lips. Caught off guard, Jake attempted to say something and when he opened his mouth, her tongue danced lightly across his lips and touched his tongue.

The kiss was erotic and explicit and Jake felt a surge of lust shoot through him that shocked him with its intensity.

This was Ashley! he reminded himself, wondering who had taught her to kiss like that. He grabbed her wrists and shoved her away from him, breathing hard and irritated with himself for not stopping the kiss sooner.

"What the hell do you think you're doing!"

She blinked slowly, as though only now becoming aware of their surroundings. Her mouth was moist from his and her eyes, when she opened them, reflected that she had also been strongly stirred by their kiss.

He was furious with both of them. She had no business kissing any man—especially him—like that. It was indecent, it was—

"Damn it, Ashley. Don't play your teenage games with me. Go find someone your own age to flirt with."

He saw the glint of tears in her eyes as she turned away. How the hell was he supposed to handle this? She'd been practicing her wiles on him, that's all. Maybe she felt safe with him, but if she did she was wrong. She was far from safe when she could turn him on so quickly.

He reached for her wrist and she stopped without turning around.

"I'm sorry, honey, it's just that—"

She tugged her arm loose and continued on her way. He heard her say, "No need to explain further, Jake. You've made yourself quite clear."

Jake turned and slowly walked back to where his brothers stood. It was obvious they had seen and heard what had happened, which didn't help his mood any.

The four of them stood there silently while Jake wrestled with his libido.

"Why are you so shocked, Jake?" Jared finally asked. "You know how she feels about you—you've been her idol all her life. You should have seen that one coming."

"That's bull and you know it. She may have had a childish crush at one time, but—"

"But nothing!" Jude stopped him. "If she had a childish crush, that crush has grown up, Jake. You didn't have to treat her like she was contagious or something."

Jake rubbed his forehead. "All right, all right. You've made your point. I could have been more diplomatic, but she caught me so off-guard that I—" He saw her reach the dance floor and sighed with resignation. "I need to go apologize."

Jake went after her, trying to come up with an explanation for his behavior that wouldn't shock an innocent girl.

He looked for her on the crowded dance floor, but didn't see her. He ran into his mom and asked if she'd seen Ashley.

"She's hard to keep track of, especially tonight." Gail glanced around before saying, "Maybe she went into the house."

He made his way through clusters of guests until he reached the house. Once inside, he frowned at the number of people there, making his search tougher. Because of the hacienda's size, it took him a while to discover that she wasn't in the house.

She was nowhere to be found.

# One

*Nine years later*

**"I'**m in and I raise you twenty-five," Jake said to Tom McCain, the president of the largest bank in town. He glanced at the others—ranchers Kent and Lew, and Curtis, a local lawyer. They were in the back room of the Mustang Bar & Grill, located on the outskirts of New Eden, for their weekly poker game.

Jake sat with his back to the wall, his chair balanced on two legs and his Stetson low on his forehead. He could hear the rowdy noise of the barroom through the thin walls. Cigar smoke eddied and circled around them, and the gathering of beer bottles on the table attested to the fact they had been playing for some time.

By upping the stakes, he would let the others know he was serious about this hand. Since they played dealer's choice, Curtis had chosen seven-card stud.

Jake had learned the small giveaway movements of each player because they had played together for years. Kent absently moved his wedding ring around his finger with his thumb when he had a good hand. Curtis whistled or hummed when he was bluffing. Jake knew that Curtis was unaware of his nervous habit.

Lew had trouble sitting still and had a habit of shifting restlessly in his chair when he couldn't decide if his hand was good enough to win. Jake carefully watched Tom, the banker, looking for possible clues. Tom never fidgeted or changed expression, which made him a tough adversary and a damn good poker player. Probably made him a good banker, as well.

Jake considered any night he bested Tom to be a good night.

Tonight looked to be one of those nights. Tom had two jacks, a ten of spades and a three of diamonds showing. His raises this hand had been strong enough to make Jake wonder if he was holding more than two pair or if he was bluffing.

There was no way to know by his demeanor, but Jake intended to find out.

Kent said, "Too rich for my blood, hombres," and tossed down his cards with a sigh.

Tom was next. He glanced at Jake over his bifocals and said, "I'll meet your twenty-five and raise you fifty."

The other two quickly folded as well.

Curtis dealt them each their last card.

There was a pile of money on the table and the three onlookers watched intently. Jake said, "I'll meet your fifty and call."

Tom studied his cards but, before he could answer, the door from the bar opened, banging against the wall, and a sea of noise swept into the room.

Neither Jake nor Tom acknowledged the intrusion.

Jake kept his eyes on Tom, wondering if he had the cards to beat him.

Jake's concentration was suddenly shattered when his cousin Jordan spoke immediately beside him.

"Sorry to interrupt, Jake, but you're needed at the ranch right away."

Jake shook his head without turning. "Not now, Jordan. Whatever it is, you can handle it."

"Wish I could, but I can't. You need to get out there. Now."

Tom smiled at Jake. "Go on, Crenshaw, I'll guard the pot," causing the other three to laugh.

"I just bet you will. If you're staying in, pay up and let me see what you have."

Tom paid, then placed his cards on the table—three jacks and a pair of tens, a full house. "I hope this teaches you something, Crenshaw," he said and reached for the pot.

"Yeah, Tom, it teaches me that I should have raised you a hundred," Jake replied, and turned the three cards he had down face up. He had a straight flush, three through seven, of clubs. He stood and reached for the money. "I hate to break this up, but as you can see, I'm needed elsewhere."

The rest of them gave him a bad time about winning and leaving immediately afterward, accusing him of planning it that way. Tom leaned back in his chair and said, "Well, hell, Crenshaw, the least you could do is give me a chance to win some of my money back!"

Jake lifted the corners of his mouth in a slight smile. "Next week, Tommy, my boy," he said to the banker. "You'll get your chance."

He finished folding the money and stuck it into his shirt pocket. For the first time since Jordan had barged into the room, Jake turned and actually looked at him.

Twenty-six-year-old Jordan was generally laid-back and low-key. Jake had never seen him this agitated before.

Jake said his goodbyes and walked into the other room, Jordan close on his heels. He continued moving through the crowd, responding to greetings without pausing, until they were outside in the graveled parking lot.

He turned and faced his cousin with considerable irritation.

"All right, Jordan, what the hell is so blasted important that you had to interrupt me at the game tonight? This is my only time to relax, kick back and enjoy myself. If the place were on fire, you would have called the fire department. If you'd spotted rustlers, you would have called the sheriff. So what, in your mind, couldn't wait until I got home?"

"Tiffany."

Jake stiffened. "What are you talking about?" His voice grew louder.

"She's at the ranch."

Jake stared at Jordan, stunned. Why would his ex-wife show up after all this time? He gave his head a quick shake. "Did she say what she wanted?"

Jordan got into his truck and slammed the door. "I'll let her explain that. Told her I'd come get you and I have. Now I'm headed home. If I hadn't been concerned about one of my mares, I wouldn't have been there when she showed up." He gave a brief wave and left.

Jake stood there, his hands on his hips, staring at the taillights until they disappeared from view. Tiffany Rogers had come back to the ranch after she'd vowed never to step foot on the place again. Wasn't that just dandy? He'd never expected to see her again and couldn't imagine what she wanted from him now.

He shook his head in frustration before he climbed

into his truck and headed toward the ranch, thirty miles from town.

What could she want—he glanced his watch—at close to midnight on a Friday night? Hadn't the woman caused him enough trouble?

He remembered the night before she left. She'd been sleeping in a guest bedroom earlier in the week, which wasn't unusual when she didn't get her way about something. By that time in their marriage, he felt he had done everything he could to make her happy and had learned to ignore her sulking. Despite her princess attitude, he'd loved her. He'd hoped that, given time, she would eventually mature into the woman he got glimpses of from time to time.

When he awakened that night and felt her in bed with him, he thought she'd gotten over her latest snit and was ready to make up. He'd sometimes wondered if she picked fights with him because she enjoyed their ritual of reconciling. Whatever her reason, he hadn't put up much resistance, he remembered ruefully.

When he'd left the house at dawn the next morning, as was his habit, he believed that everything was fine between them. When he returned to the house later that day, she was gone, having taken all her possessions as well as some of his.

Within hours, he'd been served with divorce papers. That was when he knew she hadn't been making up with him. She'd been saying goodbye.

They'd been divorced long enough now for him to recover from the shock and devastation he'd felt at the time. They'd been married almost four years when their relationship had blown up in his face.

Of course, he should have known that a Dallas socialite wouldn't be happy living in the country but she'd insisted she didn't care where they lived as long as they were together, and he had been too besotted to realize that their marriage wouldn't work. She'd said what he wanted to hear and he had believed her.

Anyone with half a brain would look at the woman and know that Tiffany Rogers of the Dallas Rogerses would never be content as his wife. He hadn't seen it at the time, probably because his brain hadn't been the part of him making his decisions. Later, during one of her frequent tirades, she'd told him the only reason she'd married him was that he was a Crenshaw—a member of one of the most wealthy and powerful families in the state.

Their divorce had been far from amicable, as the lawyers liked to call a divorce where the husband rolls over and plays dead while the wife walks off with everything. Four years hardly constituted a long-term union and his lawyer—and poker-playing friend, Curtis Boyd—had vigorously fought her when she'd asked for an outrageous amount of money for alimony. He and Curtis knew she didn't need the money. She'd just wanted to get back at him because he refused to let her stomp all over him.

The day he walked out of the courthouse a free man, he made a vow to himself never to get married again. He'd learned his lesson well. Marriage might be great for other people, but he wanted no part of it. He was content to remain a bachelor for the rest of his life.

Now she was back here for God only knew what reason, and once again he was being forced to face her.

The road to the ranch had little traffic at this time of night. He followed its winding path through picturesque hills until he had to slow for the turn into the ranch entrance.

The entrance was framed on either side by curving walls of limestone fashioned years before he was born. He and his brothers used to play king of the mountain on their broad surfaces until the time their dad caught them. Tonight, Jake scarcely noticed the entrance as he continued along the paved private road that eventually led to the main ranch house.

When he reached the house and parked, Jake noticed a black limousine sitting in the shadows beneath the trees. That would be Tiffany, all right, always traveling in style.

With an irritated sigh, Jake got out of the cab of the truck, slammed the door with a satisfying sound and strode toward a side entrance. The sharp sound of his boots on the patio echoed his impatience. He stepped inside the door that opened into the kitchen.

He stopped just inside the doorway. Tiffany sat at the kitchen bar, calmly sipping a glass of iced tea. She'd cut her hair since he'd last seen her and she had on slacks and an open-necked shirt, looking as though she were waiting for a modeling shoot, her hair and makeup impeccable.

As soon as she saw him, Tiffany slipped off the stool and faced him, smiling brilliantly. He recognized—only because he knew her so well—that she was nervous.

Smart woman.

It took a lot of nerve for her to walk into his house when he wasn't there and make herself at home.

He leaned against the doorjamb, folded his arms and waited, his eyes shaded by his hat.

Her smile dimmed.

"Hello, Jake," she said in her sultry voice.

There had been a time when that voice had done all kinds of things to him. He was considerably older and a great deal wiser now.

"What're you doing here?"

A tiny frown appeared between her brows as she fluttered her lashes in simulated surprise. "Is that any way to greet me?" she finally replied, her bottom lip sliding out enough to form a provocative pout. "Ed brought me all the way out here to see you. You could at least be polite."

"I'm not feeling particularly polite at the moment. Who's Ed?"

"Edward James Littlefield Jr."

"Never heard of him."

She made a face. "Of course not. He and his family are quite well known in the Dallas area…banking, you know."

"You haven't answered my question."

She clasped her hands together and attempted another smile, her nervousness more obvious as her bracelets jangled around her wrists.

"I brought you something."

He straightened and started toward her. "Cut out the games, Tiffany. They don't work any more. I don't want anything from you. So if that's why you're here—"

She turned and hurried across the room toward the hallway and said, "But you haven't seen what I brought you, yet," she said over her shoulder.

He strode after her. "Where the hell do you think you're going?" he asked once he reached the front foyer.

"You'll see," she replied lightly as she ran up the wide, curving staircase toward the second floor. She didn't look back.

Damn, but she was irritating! Always playing games, never saying what she actually meant. He shook his head in disgust and followed her. By the time he reached the top of the stairs, she was hurrying toward his wing of the house as if she knew he would stop her if he caught up with her.

He wanted to shake her silly. Once he reached her, he would haul her butt out of his house, but by the time he was close enough, she was already entering one of the bedrooms. Surely she didn't actually think he'd hop in bed with her, did she? He reached the bedroom door and peered inside. She stood beside the bed, her finger to her lips. A night-light that wasn't there earlier gave the room a soft glow.

When she remained silent, he walked over to where she stood and glanced at the bed.

He froze when he saw what was there. Or rather, who was there. A little girl, clutching a faded pink stuffed rabbit with an ear missing, lay there sound asleep, the covers pulled to her shoulders.

He glanced at Tiffany, wondering what she was up to now.

The child had blond curly hair and delicate features. He had no idea how old she was or why she was there.

He shook his head wearily and walked out of the room. He didn't stop until he reached the kitchen. Once there, he went to the refrigerator and reached for a beer. When Tiffany followed him into the room, he turned to face her. "What in the hell is going on, Tiffany?"

"She's your daughter. Her name is Heather and I'm leaving her here with you."

# Two

Jake looked at her in silence for several moments before he shook his head in disgust. "Very funny, Tiffany. You'll notice that I'm not laughing, however. Need I remind you that we never had children? As I recall, once we were married, you informed me that you didn't want children because pregnancy would ruin your figure."

He drank a swallow of beer and struggled to hang on to his temper. "What game do you think you're playing here? I haven't seen you in years. Did you suddenly decide that I'm an easier touch than the father of that little girl? Sorry, but that kite won't fly. I'm not paying you child support, Tiffany. You can't hang that one on me. I want you to go upstairs, get your daughter and get the hell out of my home."

It wasn't the child's fault her mother had no integrity, he reminded himself. He couldn't help but feel sorry for the little girl, given her circumstances.

He rolled the bottle he held across his forehead to cool off. What he needed was to stick his head into one of the horse troughs outside. If he stayed in the same room with Tiffany much longer, he might forget that his mama had taught him always to be a gentleman, regardless of the provocation.

Without a word, Jake walked outside and sat down at one of the patio tables.

He stared into the night. The moon was high in the sky, almost full, giving enough light to see the rolling hills beyond his home. The vista usually had a calming effect on him. He hoped it would work this time.

There was no reason to let her get under his skin like that. Getting him to react had probably been her plan all along, wanting to see what he would say and do. Well, she had her answer.

The door opened behind him. He turned his head and watched Tiffany come outside empty-handed. His jaw tightened as she walked in and out of the shadows to the table where he sat. She sat across from him, the light from the kitchen window falling across her face.

He waited for her to speak and when she didn't, he said, "Didn't you forget something? I want you *and* your little girl gone. Now."

Tiffany lifted her chin and stared back at him. He knew that look. She was ready to fight him if she didn't get her own way. Well, too bad. She could throw as many temper tantrums as she wanted to throw, but they wouldn't work. He wasn't going to take her child and pretend it was his.

"Do you remember the night before I moved out of here?"

"Are you talking about the night you crawled into my bed after I was asleep?" he asked grimly.

She smiled at him and nodded. "Yes. I wanted to

show you that you might deny me other things, but you never denied me sex."

"You made your point. Making love to you was the only thing I seemed to do that you approved of. So what?"

"Well, as things turned out, I was a little too eager that night and since you were more than half asleep, we didn't use protection. Imagine my surprise when I discovered I was pregnant." She looked down at her clasped hands, resting on the table. "Mother Nature's little joke on me." Her voice had flattened by the time she'd stopped speaking.

"And I'm supposed to believe that?"

She looked up at him, her gaze meeting his. "I really don't care what you believe. She was born nine months after that night. Do the math."

"I doubt I was the only man who was in your bed around that time."

"I refuse to get into name-calling, Jake. Regardless of what you may want to believe, your name is on Heather's birth certificate. If you have any doubts, have the tests run."

He swallowed, thinking back to that night. He'd made love to her until they were both exhausted. She was right. He hadn't used protection. He supposed the surprise would have been if she *hadn't* gotten pregnant. If he gave the matter any thought after being served with papers, he probably figured she had used protection.

In the silence between them, he could hear the night sounds, the rustle of animals foraging by moonlight, the occasional deep croak of a bullfrog, the distant sound of a dog barking. "If you were pregnant at the final hearing," he said after several minutes, "why didn't the information come out in court?"

She sounded irritated and impatient. "Because I hadn't paid attention to my monthly cycles during that horrible time. I was so distraught that I put any irregularity down to stress. The divorce was final before I discovered the truth."

Which still didn't explain why he didn't know about it. Knowing Tiffany, as soon as she found out, she would've been screaming for his head… or other, more delicate parts of his anatomy…to be removed from his body.

"Why didn't you tell me once you found out?"

"Because I didn't want to have anything more to do with you, that's why! I decided to raise her on my own. There are lots of single mothers who raise their children alone. You'd been so hateful during the divorce proceedings I decided you didn't deserve to know you were going to be a father!"

"So you decided to punish me by not letting me know, is that it?"

"Yes!"

"The only problem with your logic, Tiffany," he said wearily, "is that it isn't punishment if I didn't know about her."

If what she said was true—and it would be easy enough for him to find out—then he really was the father of the little girl upstairs.

His stomach knotted at the thought and he broke into a cold sweat. For more than three years he'd had a child that he never knew existed.

"Why tell me now? Did you figure I'd been punished enough after all this time? You've kept her very existence from me for all these years, Tiffany, including the pregnancy itself. Care to explain to me why, after all this time, you brought her here tonight?"

She shifted and appeared to be trying to decide how to answer him, clasping and unclasping her hands.

Uh-huh. This was going to be good, watching her squirm. If he could find any pleasure in this encounter, which was certainly doubtful, it would be watching Tiffany as she tried to figure a way to justify her actions, which were inexcusable. He knew she was self-absorbed and permanently immature, but he never thought she would stoop so low as to keep a child from her father in order to get revenge.

She looked away from him, chewing her bottom lip. Finally, as though answering his question, she said, "Soon after Heather was born, my schedule became so hectic that my grandmother offered to keep her for me, which worked out great for everyone. Gram had someone to entertain and play with, and I was able to spend time with Heather as often as possible without disrupting her schedule." She paused and rubbed her forehead, as though she had a headache. "The thing is, Gram had a stroke two weeks ago and she's now bedridden. She won't be able to care for Heather."

"So much for raising a child on your own, right, Tiffany? But having your grandmother raise her for you has nothing to do with why you're just now telling me about her." He raised his brow. "Or does it? Without your permanent babysitter you don't know what else to do with her, is that it?"

"No, that is not *it*!" Her calm demeanor fell away and her anger took over. "Certain things have recently changed in my life, for your information. Ed loves and respects me—something *you* never did—and he wants to marry me! We had all our plans made—we wanted to get married in Vegas and honeymoon in Hawaii, and then visit Japan and Australia. Everything would have worked out perfectly if Gram hadn't had her stroke. The timing couldn't have been worse!"

Jake stared at her in amazement. Did this woman care about anyone other than herself? There was no sign that her grandmother's illness was anything more to her than an inconvenience.

"Let me get this straight. You planned to go off for months and leave Heather with your grandmother?"

She lifted a shoulder. "She would have been fine with Gram. They got along well together. Besides, I've taken trips before. I doubt she even misses me when I'm gone."

"You must have considered the situation desperate for you to break your silence to bring her to me."

Tiffany ran her hand through her carefully coiffed hair, another indication that this meeting wasn't going the way she'd planned. He wondered what she'd expected he would do when she showed up? Welcome her and the child with open arms? Be so thrilled to discover he was a father that he'd ignore the fact she'd kept the knowledge from him for all this time?

If so, she was even shallower than he'd always thought.

In a quieter voice, she said, "I thought I'd worked everything out just fine. I told Ed that we'd have to take Heather with us."

He dropped his head to hide a smile. After a moment he looked at her and said, "I somehow doubt he was thrilled with that particular idea. Most men expect to have their bride all to themselves at that stage of their marriage."

"I thought he had accepted the idea, although taking a three-year-old on your honeymoon is certainly not what either of us planned or wanted!"

"Couldn't your mother have looked after her?"

"That's another problem, entirely. Heather won't behave for Mother."

Another proof that she was probably his. He had to admire Heather's discrimination. Tiffany's mother was just an older, even more spoiled, version of her daughter. Too bad he hadn't recognized the similarity sooner. If he had, none of this would be happening.

On the other hand, if Mrs. Rogers and her grand-daughter—and boy, he would have loved to have seen her face when she found out she was going to be a grandmother!—had gotten along, he would never have known about Heather.

Funny how life worked sometimes.

"We left Dallas this morning," Tiffany continued, intent on her story. "I thought everything had worked out just fine. Ed never said a word to make me believe he hadn't accepted the situation until we were on the road. That's when he told me he wasn't interested in raising someone else's child. He hadn't expected to become a full-time parent when he proposed to me. He assured me that he wouldn't mind if she visited us occasionally, but he didn't want her around all the time."

Tiffany appeared to have run out of steam and just sat there looking at him.

After a moment, he said in a neutral tone, "And you still plan to marry him."

She looked at him with tears in her eyes. "Please understand, Jake. I love him, really love him. He's older, more mature. I've known who he was for years but I never expected him to show any interest in me. When he did, it never occurred to me that accepting Heather would be a problem for him. He knew about her, he'd even met her once, and I thought he would adore her as much as I do." She pulled a handkerchief from her purse and carefully blotted beneath her eyes. "When he told me that, once he realized I wasn't going to leave her in Dallas, he'd arranged for Heather to stay with a professional sitter in Las Vegas while we were overseas, I was horrified. I really was. He made it clear he didn't intend for Heather to go with us and I didn't want her to stay with a stranger. I didn't know what to do."

Jake didn't know what to say. If she still intended to marry this weasel, he figured they deserved each other.

She sighed and said, "That's when I thought about you. I remembered how you were always talking about wanting children. I decided to forgive you for being so mean to me back then. I knew that Heather would be better off with her own flesh and blood for a few months, instead of with some stranger in Vegas."

Maybe the child *was* better off with him, if this was the way she was being treated. He was still having a little trouble absorbing the fact that people could be so callous to their offspring.

He leaned back in his chair, his gaze steady, and said, "You need to understand something before this conversation goes any further, Tiffany. If you intend to leave that little girl with me after not having the decency to tell me she even existed until tonight, I refuse to allow you to bounce her between us in order to suit your convenience."

She frowned at him. "I don't know what you mean, Jake. She's your child, after all. If we can make an arrangement where each of us keeps her part of the time she'll get to know both of us. I realize that I made a mistake keeping her from you. She deserves to know her father."

Damned if she didn't sound pious.

He folded his arms. "You're treating her like a toy you grew tired of playing with. So let me make myself perfectly clear. If you leave here tonight without taking her with you, or if you decide to leave her somewhere in Las Vegas once you get there—and believe me, I'll be keeping tabs on that—I'll make certain you lose all parental rights to her. You will see her only when I think she's capable of handling it."

She looked at him as if he'd slapped her. "You'd take her away from me?" she asked in horror. She started sobbing. "I should have known better than to let you know about her at all. I should have followed my instincts and kept you out of both our lives! I *knew* you were going to be hateful about this. I just knew it!"

He stood. "C'mon, I'll help you get her back to your car."

She jumped up. "No! I can't take her with us. I just can't! I want what's best for her, I really do." Tears continued to run down her cheeks and her nose glowed where she kept wiping it with her handkerchief. She twisted the beleaguered piece of cloth between her hands. "It's just so hard, Jake," she said pathetically, "you know? I don't know the first thing about taking care of her. She won't behave, she ignores what I say, and just the other day she found some cosmetics in my purse and smeared them all over her face. I know she knew better, but she did it just to spite me! I've been doing the best I can, but I just don't know how to deal with her!"

"And you think I do."

Still wringing her handkerchief, she said, "Well, at least I'll know she's with part of her family. I don't think you'll have any trouble getting along with her because you've always been good with children. This is the best thing for Heather. You'll find someone here on the ranch to keep an eye on her when you can't watch her."

Jake held his wrist up to the light. "At one o'clock in the morning? Somehow I doubt that very much."

She seemed to regain control of her emotions, long enough to blow her nose. "I'm sure she'll be okay for a day or two until you find someone to look after her." Tiffany looked around the patio vaguely, no doubt wishing she was anywhere but here. "I, uh, hadn't realized it was so late. Ed and his driver have been so patient, waiting hours for you to come home." She gave him a half smile. "Sorry if I broke up a hot date with one of the local yokels."

Despite her words, she didn't move away. Instead, she continued to stand there, warily watching him.

"I meant what I said, Tiffany. I'm not going to punish this child by moving her back and forth between us at your convenience."

Her shoulders slumped. "I know, Jake. I love her so much, but I'm really not cut out for the whole mother thing, you know? I was horrified when I found out I was pregnant after being extra careful all those years. I didn't know what to do. Gram talked me into having her, promising me to help with her, and I'm not sorry I did. Honestly, I'm not. It's just that…" She paused as though searching for words. "I've always been high-strung, and trying to deal with her has just been too much for me. My nerves can't stand the pressure day in and day out."

She dropped her eyes and slowly turned away.

He made no comment as she left the patio. She'd almost disappeared around the corner of the house when she stopped and said, "I almost forgot, Jake. I brought all the necessary papers you'll need for her—her birth certificate, a record of her shots, that sort of thing. I'd already packed them, thinking she'd need credentials to go overseas with us. I also brought her clothes and other belongings. She's familiar with them and I hope they'll help her to adjust." She looked at him through the shadows. "Goodbye, Jake. Take good care of her."

Jake continued to stand there on the patio without moving. He was numb with all that had happened tonight. In a few moments, he heard the purr of a well-tuned engine and watched as headlights swept across the driveway.

The silence of the country night returned.

Now that she'd gone, he needed to face what had happened. If Tiffany was telling the truth, he had a daughter. A daughter he'd discovered long after he'd finally accepted that he would never have a family of his own.

That was the good news. That was the great news.

The bad news was that he had a daughter who would be waking up in the morning in strange surroundings without a familiar face to reassure her that she was safe. He had a daughter who would probably be afraid of him, at least at first.

Jake rubbed the back of his neck and picked up his empty bottle. He walked into the kitchen, tossed the bottle in one of the recycling bins on hand and looked around, trying to force his mind to wrap around the idea of instant fatherhood.

A large manila envelope he hadn't noticed before lay on the kitchen bar. He sat down on the bar stool Tiffany had used and opened the envelope.

Her birth certificate was on top. Her name was Heather Anne Crenshaw and she'd been born on Sept. 28, which meant she would be four years old in a little over six weeks.

He was listed as her father.

He stared at the document until it grew blurry. He hadn't been there when she was born. He hadn't been there when she learned to sit up, to stand, to take her first step or say her first word. He hadn't been there to watch the infant turn into a little girl.

He'd already missed so much of her life.

Jake removed his hat and hung it on the rack beside the door, turned out the lights downstairs and went up to his room. After he sat on the side of his bed and removed his boots, he returned to Heather's room in his stockinged feet. She had shifted and now lay on her side, still clutching her bedraggled rabbit. He noticed several more stuffed animals sitting at the end of the bed. She looked so innocent lying there, sleeping so soundly. She had no idea how her world had changed yet again. Her great-grandmother's sudden illness must have been devastating to her. And now this.

Eventually he quietly checked the closet and chest of drawers. Yes, Tiffany had amply provided for her, he was thankful to see.

What was he supposed to do now? Come morning, this sweet-looking child was going to wake up and face new people and new surroundings. Of course she would be afraid. She would need to be dressed and fed and...

He froze. Was she housebroken? How would he know? Raised with three brothers, his only experience around little girls was watching Ashley grow up.

Ashley.

She would know what Heather needed, wouldn't she? Would she be willing to help him out for a few days? He hadn't seen much of her in the past several years, not since she'd gone off to Texas A&M, but at one time they'd been the best of friends.

He certainly needed a trusted friend about now.

Would Ashley be able to help him?

She was a doctor, wasn't she?

Sort of. She was a veterinarian. That was close enough, wasn't it?

She was a woman, besides. She'd know what to do with a little girl, since she'd been one herself.

At the moment, he didn't have many options. He was desperate. Surely she would be willing to do whatever needed to be done for his daughter.

Jake returned to his bedroom, looked up her number and called her.

# Three

Ashley Sullivan unlocked the door to her small apartment in time to hear her phone ringing. She groaned. It was the middle of the night and she was exhausted. Because this was her weekend on call, she'd already been out on two emergencies tonight, once for a mare having trouble with a breech birth and the other to check out a steer whose owner thought had been bitten by a snake. And this was only Friday night.

A call in the middle of the night was always ominous. She dropped her medical bag and grabbed the phone.

"This is Dr. Sullivan," she said, her voice weary.

"Uh, hi, Ashley."

She sank to the side of her bed, shaken by the realization of who was calling her.

When she didn't immediately respond, he added, "This is Jake Crenshaw. I hope I didn't wake you."

As if she wouldn't know the sound of his voice. Adrenaline shot through her as she thought of possible reasons he would be calling her at this time of night.

"What's happened?" she said with dread. "Is it Dad?"

"No, no. Nothing like that." He paused and she wondered what was going on. She hadn't spoken to Jake in years. "I, uh, I've got an emergency on my hands out here. I hate to ask this of you, but would you mind coming out to the ranch?"

She checked the time and winced. *"Now?"*

He cleared his throat. "I know it's late but I really need you."

"What's wrong?" She had never heard those words from Jake before and they shook her.

When he didn't answer right away, she wondered if he'd hung up. When he did answer, he was frustratingly vague. "I'd rather show you once you get here, all right?"

It was her turn to pause and think about his request. She was exhausted and therefore vulnerable. Let's face it, she would be vulnerable around him no matter when she saw him.

"I'd like to help you out, Jake, but I've been working nonstop since seven this morning. Can this wait until tomorrow?"

"No, it can't." He sounded impatient and irritable, which meant he was being his normal and oh-so-charming adult self, not the boy she'd grown up with. When she didn't reply, he said, "This is something personal. You were the first one I thought of when I knew I needed help."

Ashley put her hand over her heart and tried to breathe. She wasn't prepared for this. Someday, maybe, when she was…oh, sixty-something…she'd be able to deal with her reactions where Jake was concerned.

"I'm sorry—" she began when he interrupted her.

"I know we haven't been as close these past few years as we once were, Ashley," he said.

Ashley pulled the phone away from her ear and frowned at it in disbelief. Talk about understatement!

He continued to speak and she forced herself to listen. "I hoped that you would be willing to help me out based on the friendship we once shared."

Wasn't that just like a man? Oh, yeah, I carelessly trampled on your heart with my size thirteen boots, but, hey, you've patched it up just fine, so how about giving me another go at it.

"Jake," she began, "I really don't think—"

"Ashley," he said, suddenly sounding panicked. "I just received the shock of my life tonight. Tiffany was here earlier and told me that we have a daughter who will soon be four years old. She left her here and I haven't a clue what to do for her or about her or with her."

Ashley was glad she was sitting down. Jake had a daughter? She struggled to breathe around the sudden constriction in her throat.

"The thing is," he continued, "she's going to wake up in a few hours in a strange place to see a man she doesn't recognize." His voice deepened. "I'm hoping you'll come out and be here when she wakes up."

Oh, dear. She was definitely in trouble here. That low, intimate tone of his had always melted her heart. This conversation was not going well at all. "You mean stay at Dad's?" she finally asked.

"I mean stay here with me and Heather. That's her name, by the way. Heather Anne Crenshaw."

Ashley closed her eyes. What should she do? She was too exhausted to think straight. Being anywhere around Jake—and in his home, no less—would be so painful for her.

But this wasn't about Jake.

He has a daughter. The daughter she'd dreamed someday they would have together. Sure, she'd been a

naïve kid at the time who'd thought his casual accep-
tance of her in his life meant more than it had. Harsh
reality had set in years ago, but his having a daughter
seemed to trigger a whole bunch of memories she'd
hoped she'd buried.

"All right," she finally said, resigned to the coming or-
deal. "I wouldn't want to be the one responsible for scar-
ring her for life because she had to face you first thing in
the morning." A hint of a smile hovered on her lips.

She heard the relief in his voice. "Thank you, Ashley. I promise you won't regret this."

Oh yeah? She was already regretting it, but he'd hit
a weak spot she'd always had for children. "I'll be there
as soon as I can," she said and hung up.

She glanced down at her clothes and wearily shook
her head. After a day in the office and an evening around
large animals, she had to clean up before going anywhere. Although she'd scrubbed up at each place, her
clothes were far from clean.

Ashley walked into the bathroom and stared at herself in the mirror. She was glad she'd had her hair cut
last year, saving her precious time and worry with her
busy schedule. The short style was definitely a wash-
and-wear hairdo.

Deep shadows beneath her eyes reflected her weariness. She closed them briefly. You can do this. Dredge
up some energy somewhere and do it.

She stripped out of her clothes and stepped into the
shower, letting the water flow over her while she did her
best to make her mind blank.

Instead, more memories flooded her.

Jake at twelve, following their dads everywhere they
went, with her four-year-old self trailing along behind.
Riding in front of him in the saddle, asking jillions of
questions, making him laugh. He'd been tall for his age,

with a shock of thick blond hair that invariably looked untidy, the most gorgeous eyes that changed from a smoky blue to a silvery gray, depending on his mood, and a smile that could stop a female's heart at twenty paces.

Not that any of that registered with her at four years old. All she knew then was that she didn't want to let him out of her sight.

By the ripe old age of seven, she'd known that this was the person she would marry someday and told everyone who would listen. Now she wondered how fifteen-year-old Jake had dealt with the teasing he must have gotten back then. If he'd been embarrassed by her remarks, he'd never let on to her.

Jake had made her childhood magical. He'd taught her how to ride a horse, rope a calf and how to safely handle and shoot a rifle. He'd cautioned her never to leave the settlement alone without protection from the wild animals that lived in the hills. They'd spent many hours following various animal tracks until she could recognize what had made them and how to avoid the dangerous ones.

He'd been in college when Ashley was twelve and her mother left. As soon as he heard about it, Jake had come home to check on her and make sure she was able to cope. With his help and the ongoing concern of his family and her dad she'd eventually adjusted to being left behind.

Her childhood ended when her mother left. She wondered what she would have done during that time without her dad and the Crenshaw family.

Her love for Jake grew steadily stronger as the years went by.

She'd looked forward to her sixteenth birthday for years, having decided that sixteen was the time when she would be truly grown up, the time when Jake would see her as a woman, when he might declare his feelings for her and promise to wait for her until she was finished with school and they could be married.

A stupid dream had come crashing down the night of her birthday. Oh, he'd declared his feelings, all right, but his declaration had been nothing like she'd imagined it would be, and she'd been forced to recognize that she had been a complete fool where he was concerned.

Any lingering doubts about his feelings for her were put to rest two years later, when he married Tiffany a few weeks before Ashley graduated from high school.

She'd cried for days, trying to come to grips with her shattered dreams. Many a night she had dreamed about Jake—a penitent Jake, begging her to forgive him for the way he had treated her, promising to make up for his behavior by offering his undying love to her and begging her to marry him.

She'd gone to the wedding with her dad, despite the fact they had to drive to Dallas and stay the weekend. Her dad told her that Jake had paid all the expenses for the families living on the ranch who wanted to attend his wedding.

She would never forget the look on his face the day Tiffany walked down the aisle toward him. He'd never looked at *her* like that. That was when she knew with absolute certainty that he had never thought of her as anything more than a kid, a nuisance that he'd accepted as part of his life.

A few weeks later, she'd convinced her dad to let her begin college that summer and she had left soon after Jake and Tiffany returned from their honeymoon. There was no way she could hang around the ranch watching them together. Except for brief visits to see her dad over the years, she'd stayed away from the ranch, concentrated on her schooling and put him firmly out of her mind…or so she'd convinced herself.

Now she had agreed to help Jake care for the child of that marriage.

She was an idiot.

After drying off, Ashley pulled on a fresh pair of faded jeans and a cotton sweater, grabbed a pair of running shoes, packed an overnight bag and headed out once again, promising herself that she absolutely would not succumb to any lingering feelings she might have for the man.

It was two-thirty by the time Ashley reached Jake's home. She stopped in front of the house, parked her truck and walked toward the solid wood double doors in front.

Jake must have been watching for her because he opened one of the doors as soon as she got out of her truck and waited in the doorway as she walked toward him.

She slowed as soon as she saw him silhouetted against the light before she forced herself to continue to where he waited.

"Thank you for coming," he said, closing the door behind her. He looked as tired as she felt. He turned and led the way to the staircase. She closed her eyes briefly, glad he couldn't see her reaction to him. The deep timbre of his voice caused chills to race up and down her spine.

When she'd walked past him, he'd been close enough for her to feel the warmth of his body, to hear the sound of his breathing and to catch a faint whiff of the combination of scents that were Jake. He still used the same aftershave.

"No problem," she replied, lying through her teeth. "Where is she?"

"Up here." He started up the stairway.

This house had been her second home as a child. Jake's parents had surrounded her with their love, treating her as though she were one of their own. She hadn't expected the barrage of memories that swept over her as she followed Jake up the stairs.

You can do this, you know you can. Just because you haven't been here or this close to him in…nine years or more…is no reason to react to him now. You're not the same person. Of course, neither is he, a thought she didn't find particularly reassuring.

Once they were upstairs, Jake led the way down one of the hallways before he paused in front of a slightly open door.

She waited for him to enter. Instead, he waved her into the room without speaking.

The first thing Ashley saw when she drew closer to the bed was a mop of golden curls. Not surprising, since both he and Tiffany had blond hair. Of course, there was a good chance that Tiffany's came from a bottle.

Meow.

Heather lay on her side facing Ashley and as soon as she saw her, Ashley knew she was a goner. Her delicate features were a feminine version of Jake's.

Later, Ashley would look back on this moment and realize that she had fallen in love with Heather at first glimpse.

Heather wore bright yellow pajamas with Disney characters dancing on them and she had her arm around a rather beat-up-looking stuffed animal that might have been pink at one time.

Ashley leaned closer and replaced the light covers that Heather had kicked off, tucking them around the child's shoulders. She muttered something in her sleep and rolled onto her back, one arm flung out.

She was adorable. Of course, she was. What had she expected, with parents who looked like Jake and Tiffany?

Heather's chubby cheeks and heart-shaped face were so innocent. How could a mother abandon such a sweet child? She certainly knew how it felt to be abandoned by a mother.

Ashley stood there for several minutes, coming to terms with the fact that her life had shifted in a significant way. Regardless of what happened where Heather was concerned, Ashley's life would never be the same.

She found Jake waiting in the hallway when she walked out of the room. They retraced their steps until they reached the foyer. He motioned for her to go into a sitting area made comfortable by soft pillows on the sofas and chairs.

"She's beautiful, Jake," she said, walking to one of the chairs and sitting down. Her voice broke slightly.

"Yeah," he said gruffly. "She's that, all right." He sat down across from her.

"Tell me what happened tonight. I need to understand what I'm dealing with here. Will Tiffany be back in a few days?"

Although he sounded calm enough, the knuckles of his folded hands were white and she knew he was struggling with his own emotions.

"I arrived home tonight to find Tiffany here. She'd already put Heather to bed and had unpacked her belongings, making sure she had the advantage when I walked into the house. In a nutshell, she's getting married to some jerk who doesn't want to deal with a child. He didn't mention until after they left Dallas today that he planned to leave Heather with someone in Vegas, where they're getting married. They'd made plans for an extended honeymoon and as far as the fiancé was concerned Heather wasn't a part of those plans."

"That's terrible! How could she choose to marry a man who would abandon her child like that?"

"I gave up trying to understand Tiffany a long time

ago. I'm still coming to grips with the idea that I have a daughter and was never told about her until tonight."

Ashley stood and walked over to the large fireplace that was the focal point of the room. If she was feeling overwhelmed, she could only guess what Jake must be feeling.

He watched her in silence until she knew she had to say something. But what? "I don't see where my being here is going to help you, Jake. I'm as much a stranger to her as you are."

"I know. However, she's been with women—her great-grandmother and to some extent Tiffany—and I hope she'll feel less threatened by a woman during those first few minutes. At least, that's my hope."

"Then what, Jake? Even if I knew how to take care of a child—which I don't—I don't have time to help you with her, except for maybe a few hours in the morning. What about April? Is she still managing the house for you? Maybe she can help out."

Jake stood as well. "April has enough to do supervising the cleaning and cooking around here. And Craig would never go for the idea of his wife spending her evenings here, as well. Meanwhile, I have a daughter and not a clue about how to care for her. She's going to wake up in a few hours and I have no idea how she'll react when she finds out her mother isn't here. I admit I'm grasping at straws. I guess I hoped you would have some suggestions about what I can do."

"Why me, Jake? There are several women here on the ranch you could have called."

"The truth?" he asked, kneading the back of his neck. "Because I remember you at that age and how happy you were. I thought you might know what little girls like to do. What's important to them and all the mysterious things that I don't have a clue about where she's concerned. I have no idea what she likes to eat and drink, or if she can even dress herself. Hell, for all I know she could still be in diapers."

Ashley's heart sank at the implications. Committing to helping Jake for any length of time would be emotional suicide. And yet... she couldn't get that sweet face out of her mind.

"Jake, let's take this one step at a time, okay. I can't think clearly right now. I'm exhausted. I need sleep. My brain has rolled over and is playing dead." She stared at him, wishing she were anywhere but here. "I know this is horrendously difficult for you. However, the upside is that you've been given a precious gift. I never knew Tiffany, but the fact that she chose to have Heather is admirable."

"Yeah," he muttered. "I was surprised she went through with the pregnancy. She made it clear soon after we married that she didn't want to have children." He sounded as tired as he looked. "Perhaps if I'd known she felt that way before we married..." His voice trailed off.

"You would have married her anyway," she said, finishing his sentence. "You were so obviously in love with her," and probably still are. Hearing that Tiffany was getting married again must have been another harsh blow for him.

She was so engrossed in her thoughts that she didn't realize Jake had stepped toward her until he wrapped his arms around her and held her tightly against him, her toes barely touching the floor. "Thank you for doing this."

Oh, help. This was not good, not good at all. He was too close, too big, too male, too...Jake.

She could already feel the cracks in her heart widening. No matter what she decided, her damaged heart was already at risk.

# Four

Jake placed his hand on the back of her head and held her to his chest without speaking.

She relaxed against him, closed her eyes and wanted to cry. It wasn't Jake's fault. It was just that she was too tired to fight...him or herself.

When he released her, he cupped her face with his hands. "I had no idea how much I've missed you until I saw you tonight. It's been a long time, hasn't it?"

"Yes," she replied, not meeting his eyes. "I'm no longer the little girl who used to live here on the ranch."

He smiled his endearing, lopsided smile and gently brushed her lips with his. "Don't I know it," he said, straightening. "You've grown into a beautiful woman, Ashley."

"Thank you. We haven't spent time together in years, Jake. Don't make assumptions about who I am based on our shared past."

He stepped away. "You're right. I guess I still see you as the girl you used to be. It's past time we got reacquainted, isn't it?" When she didn't answer him, he rubbed her shoulders with his large, strong hands and said, "But not tonight." He took her hand and led her out of the room. "I'll give you your choice of bedrooms. There's one on either side of her room and one across the hallway. You can decide which one suits you." He snagged the bag she'd left at the bottom of the steps without breaking stride and continued up the stairs, still holding her hand.

It was just as well. She was almost too tired to walk.

They paused in the hallway near Heather's door while Ashley glanced into the three rooms he'd mentioned and said, "I'll take the one across from her."

"Okay. Each bedroom has its own bath. I think you'll find everything you need. If not, let me know and I'll get it for you." He handed the bag to her.

She walked inside the room and placed her bag on one of the chairs. "Your mother is going to be so thrilled to hear that she has a granddaughter," she absently commented, turning back the covers on the bed. "She once said to me that she sometimes wondered if any of you would ever settle down and produce offspring." When he didn't respond, she thought he'd left, so Ashley was surprised when she straightened to find him standing in the doorway with a startled look on his face.

"What's wrong?"

"My folks. I need to tell my folks."

"I thought they were out of town."

"They are, somewhere in the Northwest, but they check in regularly. Mom will want to rush back home as soon as I tell her."

"Nothing wrong with that. She'll be able to watch Heather for you until you can make other arrangements."

He shook his head. "I can't use her like that, Ashley. It wouldn't be fair. She deserves to travel with Dad after all these years without worrying about what's going on here. I'll figure out some other way to muddle through this." He turned away and she closed the door behind him.

Once Jake left, Ashley took a closer look at the room. The furniture looked to be lovingly cared-for heirlooms, while the furnishings were elegantly contemporary.

She slipped off her clothes and crawled into bed, barely getting the lamp off before she was sound asleep.

Jake walked into his bathroom and closed the door behind him, leaning against it. Tonight had certainly been a night of shocks for him…a definite emotional overload. Discovering that he was a father of a little girl had been a jolt; having her be his sole responsibility was another. But seeing Ashley again after so many years of casually waving when she was visiting her dad hadn't prepared him for the woman she'd become.

He turned on the shower and undressed, thinking about Ashley.

The woman who arrived tonight was a heart-stopping, alluring woman. He'd seen glimpses of the woman she would become in the teenage tomboy he'd known so well. But he'd never expected her to affect him this strongly.

He stepped into the shower and let the water beat against his tense muscles.

She was still small, but her body had filled out into breath-stealing shapeliness. The single braid she'd always worn as a kid was gone, replaced with a short boyish cut that looked anything but boyish on her. Her hair curled around her cheeks and ears, drawing attention to her exotically shaped green eyes, her high cheekbones and her long, graceful neck.

Even as a child, those eyes of hers had made it difficult for him to resist doing anything she asked.

Tonight they had been shadowed with fatigue and he'd felt like a louse for insisting she come out here at this hour. His hug and kiss had been spontaneous, expressing his relief at her willingness to help him out. He hadn't been prepared for the strong reaction that had hit him like a sledgehammer when he'd barely brushed her lips.

He was suddenly reminded of the night years ago when she'd kissed him until his head swam and his heart pumped blood to places it had no business going…at least not with Ashley! His strong reaction to her back then had horrified him as he recalled, and he hadn't handled the situation well.

She'd been a kid, experimenting with her new-found sensuality and wouldn't have understood the reaction she'd stirred in him.

He doubted she even remembered the incident now, but it had been a strong wake-up call for him to stay away from her until she was old enough to understand what was happening between them.

She was an adult now and the attraction certainly hadn't cooled off where he was concerned. With all the sudden turmoil going on in his life—had it been only four hours ago that his only concern in life was to beat Tom McCain at poker?—the last thing he needed was the added stress of dealing with his feelings for Ashley on top of everything else.

Once she prepared Heather to meet a father she didn't know and eased their first meeting, Ashley would leave and he'd be able to deal with the situation on his own.

He hoped.

He'd have to wait until Monday to call employment agencies in Dallas, Austin and San Antonio and alert them to his immediate need for someone qualified to care for his daughter.

Jake turned off the water and briskly toweled off before he returned to his bedroom. When he crawled into bed, he suddenly realized that it wasn't a good idea to continue sleeping in the nude now that his daughter was here. It occurred to him that dressing differently for bed was only the beginning of the changes he needed to make in his life now that Heather lived here.

He smiled as he closed his eyes. He was the father of a precious little girl. Any changes needed would be worth it.


Ashley had barely fallen asleep when someone shook her shoulder. She groaned and muttered, "Go away," without opening her eyes.

However, Jake's voice close to her ear was all that was needed to yank her from a sound sleep and remind her where she was.

"Ashley," he whispered. "I'm sorry to wake you but Heather's stirring. She's still in bed, but she's called for 'Gram' a couple of times. Now's she's calling for 'Mommy.'"

His voice shook as though there were a bomb ready to detonate in the next room.

Ashley rubbed her eyes and through sheer willpower forced them to stay open. "What time is it?"

"A little after six. I'll make coffee while you go talk to her."

Ashley looked at him. He was freshly shaved and wore crisp, clean clothes. How could anyone look so good this early in the morning?

As soon as he left, she threw back the covers and found her clothes.

Once dressed, Ashley opened her door and was surprised to see Jake hovering in the hallway. "C'mon, Jake," she whispered. "She's just a little girl. You're acting as though the house is about to explode or something!"

"Sorry. It's just that," he ran his fingers through his hair, "I don't want her frightened. She's so little. What if she starts crying!"

His eyes looked wild.

She shook her head. One of the roughest, toughest guys in Texas brought to a trembling halt by the fear of a child crying. Who would believe it?

"All children cry from time to time, Jake," she said patiently. "It isn't the end of the world. Go make the coffee you promised me and I'll see what I can do."

They'd been talking in low voices and she wondered if Heather could hear them. Once Jake left, she peered around the doorway and saw the little girl kneeling in the middle of the bed, her arms overflowing with stuffed animals.

Ashley took a deep breath and pasted a smile on her face. *Here goes.* "Good morning, Heather," she said cheerfully, walking slowly into the room. "How are *you* this morning?"

Heather started and turned to face her, clutching her toys closer.

"I don't know you," she said, her blue eyes round and her voice trembling. "Where's my mommy?"

To give Heather time to adjust to her presence, Ashley walked over to the window and opened the blinds, allowing the sun to flood the room. She turned and moved slowly toward the bed, sitting at the foot of it.

"My name is Ashley. Your mommy left you here last night so you could spend time with your daddy." How much of all this would a three-year-old understand? Ashley prayed for guidance to say the right things to Heather without making her more upset than she already was.

Heather looked at her for a long moment, frowning. "I don't have a daddy."

The stark words wrenched her heart. The poor baby. This was going to make the meeting with Jake more difficult than either of them had guessed.

"Sure you do," Ashley replied softly. "He's very happy that you've come here to see him and he can hardly wait to see you. You want to meet him?"

Heather looked down at her rabbit. When she raised her eyes, they glistened with tears. "I have to go to the bafroom."

"Oh, of course you do." Why hadn't she thought of that? "See that door over there? You have your very own bathroom. Do you need help?"

Heather quickly shook her head, slid off the bed on the side opposite Ashley and ran into the bathroom, firmly closing the door behind her.

Ashley's shoulders slumped. Well, that had gone well. Yeah, right. What did she know about little girls? Having been one certainly wasn't a qualification for helping a frightened little girl deal with a whole new environment.

She heard the toilet flush and water running. Someone had trained her well. When she finally opened the door, Heather was trying to pull up the bottoms of her pajamas that were in a twist with her panties.

"Need some help, sunshine?"

Heather stopped and looked up. "I'm Heather. Not sunshine."

"I think you look like a ray of sunshine in your bright yellow pajamas, your pretty blond curls and bright blue eyes. Sunshine is like a nickname, a playful name."

"Oh."

Heather solved her problem by pulling off the uncooperative apparel.

Ashley quickly got up and walked over to the

dresser. "Let's look in here and find you some clothes to wear, okay?"

Heather followed her, tugging at her pajama top. "You got clothes at your house that fit me?"

Ashley didn't believe this would be a good time to discuss ownership of the house. "Your mommy brought us yours," she replied, opening one of the drawers. Ashley pulled out a pair of navy blue pants and a pretty pink T-shirt. She could smell the enticing scent of freshly brewed coffee drifting from downstairs and mentally blessed Jake.

"How about these?" she asked, holding the shirt and pants up for inspection."

Heather shook her head. "That's not right," she said, and peeked into the drawer. When she couldn't find what she was looking for, she pulled out each of the drawers, then she reached into one of them and held up a pair of pink pants that did, indeed, match the shirt.

Heather retrieved panties and pink socks to wear with the sneakers sitting on top of the dresser.

Ashley knelt in front of the little girl, unbuttoned her shirt and slipped it off Heather's shoulders. When Heather didn't protest, Ashley held out the panties and Heather stepped into them, holding on to Ashley's arm for balance.

"Where's my daddy?" Heather whispered, looking around the room nervously.

"He's downstairs in the kitchen. We'll go see him as soon as you're dressed."

Ashley was relieved that Heather seemed to have relaxed a little by the time she had her clothes on, her shoes tied and her hair brushed. When Ashley held out her hand, Heather took it without hesitation, causing Ashley to feel as though she had achieved a giant victory.

What a darling. And certainly independent. She was

very particular about her clothes and her hair, which Ashley found amusing. She would enjoy watching Jake with her, being shown the right way to do things. Jake's daughter might well be as strong-willed as he was.

Ashley smiled at the thought. Couldn't happen to a more deserving guy.

They reached the bottom of the stairs and were headed toward the kitchen when Heather spoke. "This house is old, isn't it?" she said, looking around curiously at the Spanish wrought-iron sconces and western paintings decorating the walls of the foyer. "Is my daddy old, too?"

Ashley's lips twitched and she firmly bit down on her lower one until she could say, "Well, that depends on what you think is old," in a sober voice. Before Heather could ask another question, they entered the kitchen.

Heather stopped abruptly and stared at Jake, who was leaning against the counter across the room, sipping a cup of coffee and warily watching her. She stared at him, the silence stretching until it seemed to fill the room, her eyes enormous as she slowly took in his size.

He carefully placed his cup behind him and went down on his haunches so that he was on her level.

The first words Jake heard his newfound daughter utter were, "You got boots on." She pointed to his feet.

He blinked and glanced quickly at Ashley before focusing on Heather once again. "Uh, yes, I do," he replied, softly. "You certainly look pretty in pink. Are those cartoon characters on your shirt?"

"Uh-huh." Heather continued to grip Ashley's hand, leaning against her leg while she studied Jake with a great deal of interest, which was a good sign, in Ashley's estimation. At least she didn't appear to be afraid of him.

"I don't have a daddy." As though to clarify her statement, Heather added, "Mommy said so."

Ashley saw a muscle flex in Jake's jaw and his eyes narrow, but when he spoke his voice remained soft. "Maybe your mom forgot, honey, because I'm really your dad." His voice broke on the last word.

Heather looked around the large kitchen. "Do you live in this old house?"

Jake slowly smiled. "That's right. I've lived here all my life."

"I bet you're really old, aren't you?"

"To you, maybe, although this house is older than I am."

Heather was quiet, then, until she looked up at Ashley and whispered, "I'm hungry."

Ashley had been watching Jake and when he glanced at her once again, she gave him a discreet thumbs-up gesture.

Jake sucked in some air and slowly exhaled. "Okay." He looked around as though expecting to find food on the table. "I bet I have something here you'd like to eat." He didn't sound all that sure but he walked to the pantry and looked inside. "Let's see. I have cereal and oatmeal—"

Heather wrinkled her nose in disgust. "Yuck. I hate oatmeal."

"Okay. Then I have—"

"Can I have pancakes?" she asked hopefully, looking at Ashley. She smiled winningly.

Ashley laughed. "Does that work on your mother, sunshine?"

Heather grinned. "Mommy don't feed me. Gram does. But mommy says I can't stay at Gram's anymore 'cause she's sick."

"What does Gram feed you for breakfast?"

Heather gave a quick shrug. "You know, cereal and eggs and stuff, but sometimes she makes pancakes."

"I tell you what," Ashley said, hoping to move things

along. "I'll make us some eggs, toast and bacon and we'll leave the pancakes for another morning. How's that?"

"I won't be here another morning. Mommy will come get me 'fore then."

Ashley and Jake exchanged gazes. When he didn't say anything, she turned her attention to Heather and said, "Why don't you sit at the table and I'll get breakfast going."

Easier said than done, she thought. She had no idea where to find anything and wondered if April worked on Saturdays, or if she made breakfast for Jake at all.

Ashley went to the refrigerator and was relieved to find it well-stocked.

By the time food was on the table, Jake had constructed a makeshift booster seat for Heather from a couple of thick phone books. Heather waited in the middle of the kitchen until Ashley was ready to sit down and then held her arms up to her. She had kept a careful distance from Jake since she'd first seen him. This was going to take time, Ashley knew, and she could only imagine how Jake must feel about his daughter's wariness around him.

He watched without expression while she lifted Heather onto the pile of books, which was across from Jake's place. "There you go," she said, pulling the chair closer to the table before she sat down next to her.

"You don't talk," Heather said conversationally to Jake after he'd sat down and Ashley had placed some food on Heather's plate.

"Sometimes I do," Jake said slowly. "When I have something to say."

"I always have sum'ping to say," she replied with a wise nod.

"I'm beginning to understand that." He took a bite of food, looking a little harried.

They were almost through eating when Jake said, "Da—darn it! I just remembered that I'm supposed to meet Jordan at the bank at ten o'clock. I promised him I'd be there for a meeting he's scheduled with Tom McCain." He rubbed his forehead as though getting a headache.

Oh, dear, what now? This was the time she'd planned to wave goodbye to the Crenshaw duo and let them sort out their situation on their own. Since he didn't intend to ask April to help him out with Heather, Ashley had a sinking sensation that her services were going to be needed today, as well. She couldn't imagine Heather being content to sit still for a business meeting. For that matter, neither would she.

She glanced at Heather, who really had been hungry. She'd eaten her scrambled eggs, two pieces of bacon and was presently munching on toast in between humming some kind of tune.

Now that Jake mentioned it, she recalled Jordan telling her earlier in the week that he had applied for a loan in order to build a second horse barn at his place, rather than to continue to use Jake's facilities. All of Jordan's cash was tied up in keeping his stud farm and boarding operation running.

Making up her mind—and what real choice did she have, anyway?—Ashley smiled at Heather and said, "How would you like to come with me this morning?"

"Where?"

"To where I work. I'm an animal doctor. Do you like kittens and puppies?"

"Gram says they're too messy."

"Well, they can be. If you want to come with me I could show you some."

Heather looked at her uncertainly before she glanced at Jake. "What's he going to do?" she asked as though he couldn't speak for himself.

"Well, he'll be going to a meeting and afterwards," she paused to look at Jake in a silent question, "he'll come pick you up and bring you home."

"This isn't home," Heather reminded her. "When's my mommy coming back?"

Jake tensed. "That's a good question, honey. We can talk about that once I pick you up, okay?"

Heather nodded thoughtfully. "Okay," she finally said.

"Good," Ashley said, rising. She helped Heather down and took her to the sink where she washed her hands for her. While Heather wandered around the room exploring, Ashley walked over to where Jake stood pouring himself another cup of coffee. "Are you going to be okay with her?" she asked quietly.

"I'll do the best I can under these circumstances. I appreciate your taking her with you today. I never gave the meeting a thought last night."

"You had a few other things on your mind, as I recall. It's okay, Jake. Wendy can help me with her."

"Wendy Modean? She's working for you and Woody Morris now?"

"She was the first one to show up when we advertised for office help. Now that her kids are grown, she said she's bored sitting at home."

"Well, I'll be darned. You lucked out. You couldn't have found anyone as competent as she is. I understand she worked at the bank years ago and was one of the best employees there, according to Tom. You got yourself a business professional."

"I know. She's been a lifesaver as we take on more and more clients." She glanced at her watch. "I need to go. So we'll see you around eleven or so?"

"No later than twelve, for sure." He touched her arm. "Thank you." His expression held gratitude and…something more. Ashley remembered the hug and brief kiss they'd shared last night and clamped down on her emotions. She could do this. A few more hours and she'd be done with the Crenshaws. Thank goodness. Another look from Jake like that one and she'd be throwing herself at him and begging him to love her!

She'd already learned that lesson the hard way, and she'd learned it well.

# Five

Most people considered Jake to be a strong, courageous man who met life head-on without hesitation. No one would dare call him a coward, either to his face or behind his back. He could face down man or beast without flinching.

So how could a pint-size little girl reduce him to quivering jelly?

He stood in the driveway, his hands in his back pockets, and watched Ashley drive away with Heather strapped into the backseat of the truck, both of them seemingly content with today's hasty arrangement. Before they left, Ashley suggested he get a car seat first thing, a booster seat for the table and whatever else a child that age needed.

Well, how in the world would he know?

He shook his head at the feeling of inadequacy that engulfed him and, once they were out of sight, returned to the house to wait for April. She needed to know about the sudden change in the size of his family.

April's shock when he told her about Heather was the reaction he knew he'd get from everyone. By the time he'd explained as much as he could to her, the two women who came to clean and do laundry had arrived and April told them his news.

The delay caused him to be running late.

On the way to town, Jake made a mental list of what he needed to accomplish today. He didn't think he could handle Heather on his own just yet. She was still too wary of him. For good reason, of course. He hoped that Ashley would consider helping him with Heather for a day or two, just until he felt easier about looking after her.

A sudden picture of Ashley asleep this morning interrupted his train of thought. He'd opened the door and quietly called to her, careful not to let Heather hear him. Unfortunately Ashley hadn't heard him, either.

He'd walked into the bedroom and paused, shaken by her beauty. He'd seen her asleep many times as a child but if he'd needed a reminder that she was no longer a child, the glimpse of her lying there had given it to him.

A slight scent of perfume had lingered in the room. He had taken a deep breath. Ashley. The perfume smelled of flowers and summer days. He still remembered the tomboy who once would have scoffed at the girlie stuff women wore.

He'd reached for her shoulder, feeling the delicate bones beneath his fingers.

"Go away," she had mumbled.

"Ashley," he'd said a little louder. "You need to wake up. Heather's awake."

Those thick eyelashes of hers had fluttered and her eyes had slowly opened. She'd stared at him sleepily.

He found her tousled hair and rumpled look sexy as hell. The thought of waking up each morning beside her suddenly flashed through his mind and scared him.

After his retreat to the kitchen, he'd spilled some of the coffee grounds putting them into the filter and splashed water on the counter.

He didn't know who was affecting him more at the moment—Heather or Ashley. Right now, he needed to keep his mind on Heather and off Ashley.

Jake drove around the courthouse square of downtown New Eden and parked in front of the bank. Jordan got out of his truck when Jake pulled up beside him.

"I'm sorry to be late," he said, striding toward the front door of the bank. Jordan grinned as he matched his steps to Jake's. "We're okay on time, I think." He gave Jake a speculative look. "So, big daddy, how's life treatin' you?"

# Six

"Where are we?" Heather asked from the back seat when they parked behind the animal hospital.

"We're in New Eden and this is where I work," Ashley replied, getting out of the truck. She opened the back door and unstrapped Heather. Heather held out her arms in such a trusting gesture that Ashley had to swallow the lump that suddenly formed in her throat.

She reached for Heather and swung her to the ground.

Heather looked around. The office was on the edge of town, with only a few businesses around it.

"Is it a town?"

"Yes."

"It don't look like a town."

"Probably not, considering what you're used to." She took Heather's hand and guided her to the side door.

"You won't have to stay here very long, you know. Before you know it, your daddy will be here to pick you up."

"Why?"

Ashley paused in mid-stride. "Why, what, sunshine?"

"Why is he coming to pick me up?"

"So you can go back home with him."

"But I want to stay with you," Heather explained in a patient voice.

Oops. "We'll talk about that a little later."

Ashley walked into the reception area, grateful to see that Wendy was already there.

Here was the woman who ran the office and helped Ashley and Woody Morris hang on to their sanity.

Wendy glanced up absently from some paperwork on her desk and was already looking back down when her head snapped up again in surprise.

"Is there something you've been hiding from us, Ashley?" she asked with a grin, coming around the counter to get a closer look at Ashley's companion.

Heather clutched Ashley's hand and leaned against her leg in the same bashful way she had when she met Jake.

"Heather, this is my very good friend, Mrs. Modean. She has a granddaughter just about your age named Mary Ann." Ashley turned to Wendy. "Mrs. Modean, may I introduce you to Ms. Heather Crenshaw?"

Wendy's brows drew together. "Crenshaw? From which family?"

Ashley could picture the wheels churning in Wendy's head. To save time, she answered without comment, "Jake's daughter."

"Oh! Well. What a surprise." Wendy gave Ashley an assessing look before she held out her hand to Heather and said, "How do you do, Ms. Crenshaw."

Heather, still leaning against Ashley, timidly held out her hand. "Fine," she said shyly. Wendy straightened and gave Ashley a big grin. "This is so interesting, whichever way you want to look at it. Jake with a daughter…and you looking after her."

"Just helping out a friend," Ashley replied blandly. She turned to Heather and said, "Are you ready to go look at some of our visitors in the back room?"

Heather nodded, looking around the front office. The walls were covered with drawings made by a preschool class in New Eden. They had drawn pictures of their pets. Ashley and Woody had a local artist carefully reproduce the pictures large enough to be seen and admired by all.

Wendy noticed Heather's interest and asked, "Do you like to draw, Heather?"

"Uh-huh."

"Well, when you get through looking at the animals in the back, you can come up here with me and I'll have some pencils and paper for you to use."

Ashley mouthed a grateful thank you and led Heather into the back.

The various dogs and cats that vocally greeted them in a cacophony of sound immediately enthralled Heather. Roy, one of the high school boys who helped out on Saturdays, joined them in the back area. After the necessary introductions, she told Heather she had to go out front for a moment. Heather was too engrossed in a litter of motherless puppies to care, so Ashley left Roy to keep an eye on her.

When she returned to the front, Wendy said, "If I'd known she was coming, I could have brought some of the coloring books I keep around the house for my grandkids." She eyed Ashley thoughtfully. "So. How come I never heard anything about Jake Crenshaw having a daughter?"

Ashley chuckled. "Gee, Wendy. I don't know. You must be slipping."

"Must be. She's a cute little thing, isn't she?"

"Yes. Now that she's a little more comfortable around me, I've discovered she's quite a talker."

"How long have you known her?"

"Not long."

"Sure looks like a Crenshaw, I'll give you that."

"That she does."

"Is it possible she's Tiffany's daughter?"

"Absolutely."

"Wonder why Jake never mentioned having a daughter?"

"Well, Jake's a man of few words."

Wendy leaned back in her chair, smiling. "I can remember when he used to haul you to town with him when you weren't much older than Heather, the two of you hitching a ride from the ranch with one of the hands to pick up supplies. You were always so cute, tagging along with him. I recall how patient he was with you, despite the incessant questions you were generally asking. None of the rest of us could keep up with you."

"Yep, that's me. As faithful as a hound and twice as vocal." She scanned the appointment book for today to see how busy she was likely to be.

"You know, it's funny how things work out," Wendy mused. "Somehow I always figured that once you grew up, Jake would end up married to you. Instead, he upped and married some socialite from Dallas. I never could figure that one out."

"I'm not his type, Wendy. I couldn't be more opposite in looks and temperament from Tiffany. She's big city and I'm pure country."

"You notice they're no longer married, though," Wendy pointed out with raised eyebrows.

"Not because Jake wanted out of the marriage, I'm sure. Remember, she was the one who left."

"Well, she never made much of an effort to fit in around here, as I recall. Always flitting back and forth to Dallas in that flashy fire-engine red convertible Jake bought her."

Ashley glanced at the clock. "I've got to get to work. If you know of anyone who could stay out at Jake's and take care of Heather until he can hire someone permanently, be sure to mention it when he comes in to pick her up, okay? In the meantime, you might give him some pointers on how to care for a three year old."

"You still haven't explained why you're the one who's helping him."

"Good question, Wendy. I'm not really sure about that myself."

It was close to noon when Wendy buzzed Ashley on the intercom and said, "Jake's holding on line two."

Ashley had just finished giving two Australian shepherd puppies their checkups and first shots for one of the ranchers in the area. She was washing up when Wendy called her. Woody had called earlier to say he wouldn't be in today because he'd pulled a muscle in his back. As a result, she'd been busier than she'd expected to be and hadn't had a chance to check on Heather to see how she and Wendy were getting along out front. At least she hadn't heard screaming or crying from either one of them.

Since Wendy had raised several kids of her own, Ashley had counted on her expertise to keep Heather entertained.

Other than asking a gajillion questions on their ride into town this morning, Heather had been well behaved—for a curious three-year-old—and Ashley knew things could have been much worse. What if Heather hadn't wanted to stay at the animal hospital? What if she'd demanded her mother? The possibilities didn't bear thinking about.

She reached for the phone. "Sorry to keep you holding, Jake. It's been a little hectic this morning. Are you about ready to pick her up? I'm going out in the field this afternoon to a few places, including stopping by your place to check on one of Jordan's pregnant mares."

"Actually, I'm at the hospital."

"Oh, no! What's happened? Were you in an accident?"

"Red Malone fell into one of the canyons and was banged up some. A few of the hands got him back to the house and Ken called me on my cell phone to tell me he was bringing him in. I haven't been able to talk to a doctor yet, so I don't know how serious it is. I'm not going to be able to leave until I know something."

"Of course not." She thought for a moment. "I suppose Heather can come with me on my rounds. Since I'll be at your place, anyway, I'll make the ranch my last stop and stay with her until you get there."

She heard his sigh of relief. "Thanks, Ashley. That's one less responsibility to worry about."

"Give Red my love. I hope his injuries aren't too serious."

"I second that," he replied and hung up.

When Ashley walked out front, she found Heather asleep on a pile of blankets beside Wendy's desk.

"Whose blankets?" Ashley asked in a quiet voice.

"Oh, I had Lurline run some things over that belong to Mary Ann. Since Ed and Lurline are looking to have more family, I figured she might have saved some things." She pointed to a box. "Lurline also brought one of her extra car seats for Heather until Jake can pick one up on his own. Mary Ann's already grown out of it, so Lurline's in no hurry to get it back."

Ashley could have hugged her. "What a relief. Tell

Lurline how much I appreciate it. Jake's at the hospital with Dad. Red Malone got hurt this morning and they're waiting to hear how he's doing, so I'll have Heather with me this afternoon. By the way, I didn't hear any loud voices out here this morning. How'd she do?"

"Just fine. Lurline brought a coloring book with crayons and a couple of dolls for her to play with. Heather seemed to be content with them. I also read to her whenever I had time." She held up a children's book. "She seemed to enjoy watching your patients come in and out. She really wasn't much trouble. Didn't even resist my suggestion that she take a nap, once I convinced her you wouldn't go off and leave her."

"I'd appreciate it if you would help me install the car seat before I wake her."

Wendy chuckled. "Good as done."

While they were outside, Ashley said, "She must be starving by now. I wonder what I should feed her?"

"Lurline brought over some snacks and juice when she came by. If you can wait, I'll make a list of things she'd probably like to eat."

Ashley had lucked out. "Wendy, once again, you're a lifesaver. As long as you're at it, let me know what else you think a three-year-old might need and we'll go shopping before we leave town."

After getting Heather into the seat without fully waking her, Wendy said, "She told me some very interesting things this morning." Her eyes were twinkling. "I'd love to know if even half of 'em are true."

"There's no telling." She started the motor. "I'll see you Monday."

"Hope you get some rest before you start in again next week."

"I fully intend to. Once I get home this afternoon, I'm

going to sleep until I get an emergency call. Keep your fingers crossed there won't be many of them this weekend."

After their shopping trip, she and Heather headed out of town on her first call. She should be at Jake's place by three and home asleep by four.

She could definitely use the down time after the emotional turmoil she'd been through during the past several hours. She would not have thought that anything could make her agree to spend time around Jake Crenshaw.

Except for a bright-eyed angel child who belonged to him.

# Seven

Jake glanced at his watch as he strode out of the hospital and swore beneath his breath. It was already past seven o'clock. Ashley—who had been reluctant to do more than ease his first meeting with Heather—had been responsible for Heather the entire day.

He called his house as he got into his truck. When his answering machine came on, he said, "Ashley, if you're there, please pick up."

She came on the line. "I'm here."

"I'm leaving the hospital now and will be there as soon as I can."

"Okay. I've been wondering whether I should go ahead and feed Heather, but I think she can wait another half hour."

"Damn. I forgot that she'd need to eat something! How did you feed her today?"

"Wendy was a big help. She gave me a list of kid-friendly meals and other items she might like. I picked them up before we left town."

"Remind me to fall on my knees and thank you as soon as I get there."

"Well, if you insist."

He laughed, the first time he'd felt like laughing all day.

"How's Red?" she asked.

"He's out of surgery. Besides a broken leg, he had a ruptured spleen and plenty of scrapes and bruises. Doc says he'll have no permanent damage once his leg heals. I stayed with Amy until we found out."

"I know. Dad told me when he stopped in earlier, so I'm not all that surprised that you're just now getting home."

"I'll see you soon."

"Oh, Jake?"

"Yeah?"

"Jordan was over the moon this afternoon. Said you were a big help in his getting his loan."

"All I did was lend moral support. He'll have no trouble paying a loan back, not with the business he's already built up."

"I think it was a nice thing for you to do. I'll see you."

He hung up smiling and headed out of town. It occurred to him on the way that he hadn't asked how Ashley had managed today with Heather. He'd been too wrapped up in his own day. Probably why he was divorced. There were times he struggled to juggle his responsibilities and sometimes, despite his best intentions, he still dropped the ball. This was one of those times.

Making his daughter his first priority was another one of the things he had to concentrate on. He had to remember that he had a family now.

Speaking of family, his call to Ashley had been so domestic, he cringed at the memory. "Sorry I'm late, hon, how was your day?" kind of thing. Shades of married life!

The best thing about today was that it was almost over. He could relieve Ashley and let her get back to her own routine. For all he knew, she could have a date tonight.

He frowned. He wasn't sure why the thought bothered him. She was a single, attractive—make that very attractive—woman. It would be strange if she weren't dating, especially on a Saturday night.

When Jake entered the kitchen, he caught a savory scent of something cooking. He paused in the doorway and looked around. Heather sat at the table in a new booster seat busily coloring in a coloring book. Ashley had her back to him while she leaned over and took something out of the oven.

The absolute last thing he needed to see at the moment was the enticing view of Ashley's shapely backside in those tight jeans. No matter how tired he was, he certainly wasn't immune to the fact that she was a fine-looking woman.

"That man's here," Heather announced, when she looked up from her coloring and spotted Jake.

Ashley set a steaming casserole on top of the stove and turned. "Ah. There you are. Perfect timing. We're just about ready to eat."

He nodded, strangled by the lust that had grabbed him when he first saw her.

She looked at Heather. "That wasn't a very nice way to greet your daddy, you know."

Heather tucked her chin to her chest and didn't say anything.

"I'll go wash up," Jake finally managed to say before leaving the room.

By the time he returned, he'd given himself a stern talking to about inappropriate thoughts and keeping better control of his reactions to her.

Once they were seated, Jake said, "This is wonderful, Ashley. I really appreciate your feeding us tonight."

"Actually, April had the casserole prepared when we got here. All I had to do was pop it in the oven. She said she made enough for the two of you to eat tomorrow since she's off on Sundays. I'll put what's left in the fridge before I head on home."

Heather looked at her with dismay. "Don't leave, Ashley."

Ashley smiled at her. "I have to, sweetie. This isn't my house. I live in an apartment in town. Maybe you and your daddy can come visit me there sometime. Would you like that?"

Heather stared at her with a horrified look, her lip quivering. Ashley smiled gently at her. "After you eat, I'll give you a bath and get you ready for bed before I go, if you'd like. Okay?"

Heather shook her head no and tears rolled down her cheeks. "Please don't go, Ashley," she whispered, her voice shaking. "I'll be good, I promise. Please don't leave me."

Jake's throat closed with sudden emotion. Those two had certainly bonded today while he was racing around putting out fires. Ashley glanced at him before taking Heather's hand. "You'll like staying here with your daddy, you know. When I was a little girl your age, he used to take me riding on his horse. There's all kinds of fun things to see on a ranch—horses and cows and sheep and goats."

Heather leaned her cheek on Ashley's hand and whispered, "I want to stay with you." She began to sob.

Ashley gave him a pleading look. He knew he had to say something, but what?

"Heather? Honey, listen to me, okay?" Jake said.

Ashley patted Heather's cheeks with a tissue and

Heather slowly raised her head, those blue eyes of hers looking desolate. He felt like some kind of monster.

"I want my mommy," Heather said, hiccupping.

If he could have gotten his hands on Tiffany right about now, he would have cheerfully wrung her neck. Poor baby. How could he explain what had happened without causing her to feel more abandoned than she already felt?

"I hope you aren't afraid to stay here with me, Heather," he finally said. "I'll take good care of you."

She gave a hitching sob and her tears fell faster than Ashley could dry them. "I want my Gram," she whispered.

Jake's heart sank. "Honey, your Gram is really sick, remember?"

"When's mommy coming to get me?"

"Well, the thing is, your mommy has gone on a long vacation," he began, racking his brain for a way to explain to a three-year-old why her dad had taken over parenting her.

"I could go on a bacation, too," Heather whispered to her plate.

She was breaking his heart and he had no idea how to console her.

Ashley spoke up without looking at him. "I have an idea," she said cheerfully. "Maybe we could have a sleepover tonight. I don't have to go to work tomorrow so I could stay here tonight. After your bath, we could read books until you get sleepy. Would you like that?"

Jake held his breath. Ashley was offering him an eleventh-hour reprieve and he prayed Heather would be willing to accept it.

They both watched Heather. Her cheeks were red from crying and Ashley continued to wipe her nose and face. Her tears undid him. How could he look after her when a tear could effectively bring him to his knees?

Heather finally nodded. "Uh-huh."

Ashley looked at Jake, her brows raised in a silent question. He silently mouthed "thank you" to her.

"But first, we have to clean our plates." She passed the casserole to Jake with a smile. He automatically took it, but his appetite was gone. He took a ragged breath, wondering how he could be expected to know how to comfort his daughter when he had no parenting skills.

Thinking out loud, he said, "As far as I'm concerned, Ashley can stay here every night." Could she understand how helpless he felt and how much he needed her support?

Her face suddenly bloomed bright red and he realized how his remark must have sounded to her. Man-oh-man. He was way over his head here, with both of them and sinking fast. He tried to think of some way to correct the impression he must have given her when Ashley spoke.

She reached for her glass of tea and said, "Let's deal with this night, okay? We can discuss the matter later," she said to no one in particular. She took a long drink and applied herself to the meal.

He hadn't meant to put her in a corner. She was right. They needed to talk once Heather was in bed and decide what he could do to help Heather adjust to all the changes taking place in her life.

Once they finished eating, Jake helped Ashley clean the kitchen. He couldn't help but notice that he and Ashley fell into a rhythm of doing chores together as if they'd been doing them for years.

Some time later, Jake watched Ashley bathe Heather, another routine parenting task he hadn't a clue about how to handle. Once she had put Heather to bed, he sat down and listened while Ashley attempted to read to

Heather amid a barrage of questions from the little girl about the pictures on each page.

He was lost in deep thought when he realized that Heather was talking about him. "Does he read?" she asked, and Jake tuned in on the conversation going on across the room.

"Does who read, sunshine?" Ashley asked, looking at Jake.

Heather nodded toward Jake. "Him."

"You mean your daddy?"

"Uh-huh."

"Maybe you could ask him."

Heather looked at him for what seemed to Jake like an hour before she asked with skepticism, "You aren't *really* my daddy, are you?"

"Yes, ma'am, I really am."

"Mommy tol' me Mr. L'lefield was going to be my daddy."

He kept his gaze steady. "Well, when he marries your mother, he'll be your stepfather, so that's probably why she told you that."

"Mama said we're going on a long trip with Mr. L'lefield and for me to be good while we was on our trip. I was good but I fell asleep. When I woke up I was here."

He cleared his throat, praying that he would say the right thing. "Here's the thing, sweetheart. Your mom was afraid to take you on such a long trip so she decided to let you stay with me. That way we can get to know each other. Wouldn't you like to do that?"

She gave him another one of her level stares and he realized he'd seen that same expression in every photograph ever taken of him. He found the stare a little daunting when aimed at him and had a sudden flash of sympathy for his parents.

"Can I ride a horse? And play with your dogs? And

go swimming at the creek like Ashley did when she was little?"

Jake felt an overwhelming sense of relief. She sounded more like the Ashley he'd known as a child.

"I think we can arrange that. As for a dog, one of the workers has a bit—a mama dog who had some puppies last week. We can visit his place and maybe he'll let you pick out one."

Her eyes grew wide. "Really? For my very own?"

"Yep."

Heather turned to Ashley and said, "Did you hear? I can get a puppy like the ones you have at your work."

"Sounds like fun," she said, grinning at Jake. "Nothing more entertaining than housebreaking a dog and discovering that they like to chew on everything they see."

Heather frowned. "Would they chew on my fingers?"

"A little, maybe. Mostly they chew on boots and shoes, socks and anything else left on the floor. You and your dad are going to have sooo much fun training a little puppy." She winked at Jake.

Jake rubbed his neck. The pups wouldn't be weaned for another month. Maybe that would give him some time to adjust to the idea.

"Would you like to have a birthday party?" he asked.

"With balloon animals and magic and clowns and—"

"I'm not sure we can have all of that. What I've been thinking," he paused and looked at Ashley, wondering what *she* was thinking, before saying, "we could have a big party on your birthday and have some barbecue and maybe some hot dogs and hamburgers and we could invite my mom and dad and your uncles and cousins. We'd put lights in the trees and…" He stopped and looked beseechingly at Ashley.

"Once upon a time," she said to Heather, "we had a big party here for *my* birthday. There was music and games and dancing. It was so much fun. I bet you'd have fun, too."

Jake stared at her. "I remember that party well."

She looked at him without expression. "I remember everything about that party, too." She returned her attention to Heather and said, "Guess what, Heather?"

"What?"

"It's your bedtime."

"Uh-uh."

"In fact, you were supposed to go to sleep while I read to you, instead of asking all those questions." She hugged her close and said, "Let's make a final stop in the bathroom and get a drink of water so you can go to sleep."

Heather thought about the suggestion and finally nodded. "Awright. You're going to be here when I wake up, aren't you?"

Ashley thought about this morning when Heather had awakened in new surroundings. "Of course I am."

Heather slid off the bed, took Ashley's hand and they made their rounds. When they returned, Jake was no longer there. Heather picked up her pink rabbit and crawled into bed. Ashley gave her a hug and a kiss, tucked her into bed and said, "I'll be across the hall if you need me during the night."

She turned out the light, leaving the night-light to soften the darkness.

Ashley found Jake in the living room, standing at the picture window and looking out into the evening. He'd slipped his hands in his back pockets, a habitual stance for him, and stood as though braced for the next unexpected wave to hit him.

She couldn't say she blamed him.

He had no idea how his familiar stance caused a rush of awareness to sweep over her.

"I know I should have checked with you first before telling Heather I'd stay the night," she said quietly. "It was an impulsive suggestion that I hope hasn't made things more difficult for you."

He turned at the sound of her voice. A small lamp near the sofa was on, leaving his face in shadows. He slipped his hands out of his pockets and came toward her.

"And I shouldn't have blurted out that you could stay forever. I'm sorry if I put you in an awkward position. It's definitely time for us to discuss the present situation." He motioned to the sofa. Once she sat down, he sat at the opposite end.

She waited for him to speak.

He leaned forward, his hands clasped between his knees. Without looking directly at her, he said, "I appreciate your help more than I can possibly say. I understood why you offered to stay tonight. Heather needs something or someone here who she feels she can trust and she's made it clear that person isn't me. I have to face reality. Her life has been turned upside down as much as mine has. It's a blessing she's taken to you so quickly."

Ashley couldn't remember ever seeing Jake this upset. Her heart went out to him. "You've done everything you can, which she'll understand once she's older. She did a lot of talking today while I made my rounds. I gathered that she seldom saw her mother for more than a brief visit once in a while. Most of her conversation was about the things she and her Gram did together."

Jake shook his head, his mouth grim.

"She quotes her Gram on everything from brushing her teeth, eating with her mouth closed, being polite and the reasons she's supposed to take a bath every day. I'm impressed that at her age she remembers them so clearly. It's obvious her great-grandmother has been a very good influence in her life. She's a very well-mannered child." She smiled, recalling their afternoon together. "Of course when Heather's tired, she's not quite so manageable."

When he didn't respond, she decided to remain silent. There was nothing more she could say to comfort him.

When he spoke, his voice shook. "What am I going to do, Ashley? When I went to town Friday night I had no responsibilities other than running this ranch. My life had mellowed out and I was content. I had no idea what was in store for me when I got home. I'm not equipped with the knowledge to care for her. I've never felt quite so helpless before. My world is spinning out of control. Where do I start in order for her to feel that this is her home?"

She moved closer to him and touched his clasped hands. "Love her, Jake. That's what she needs from you; that's what you can do for her."

He straightened and turned to her, his expression reflecting his pain. "And how do I do that when she won't have anything to do with me?"

When she started to move her hand away, he clasped it in his. His touch was so familiar to her. How many times had he been there to comfort her when she'd needed someone? Now it was her turn to help him.

"I know that this situation isn't going to be worked out in a day or two," she said quietly, "but you could plan things the two of you could do together. For instance, set up a routine where you read to her every night. I stopped by the bookstore before we left town today and bought several books for children her age. That should get you started."

"She's afraid of me," he muttered, looking away from her. "She's made that obvious."

Ashley tightened her grip on his hand in silent sympathy. "That's not fear, really. She's shy around you, that's all. A father is something new in her life. Give her some time to get to know you, Jake. She's a well-adjusted child and isn't afraid to meet new people, which is a good indication she's been well-treated and loved. She'll come around."

He sighed. "I appreciate your optimism. I just wish I could share it."

"I've enjoyed getting to know her. She's a character. Shy one moment, chatty the next. I know you're going to enjoy her once the two of you spend time together."

"It's the meantime that concerns me at the moment." He took both her hands in his, stroking the back of her hands with his thumbs. He looked up, his eyes silver in the muted light around them. "Since she's comfortable with you, I was wondering if you'd be willing to spend the next few nights here…just until I can figure things out. I'll find someone to live here permanently as soon as possible. In the meantime, I think she and I might be able to muddle through during the day if she knew you'd be here at bedtime and breakfast."

"It's worth considering, I suppose," she said slowly.

"I know it's not what either of us planned when I called you last night. I'm sorry for that."

"I know, Jake."

Sitting this close to him, she felt the magnetic pull he'd always had for her.

"Thank you for being so understanding, Ashley." The gentle look he gave her mesmerized her. This was Jake and he needed her. How could she say no?

And then he kissed her.

He was just expressing his gratitude, she nervously reminded herself, but the kiss slowly escalated into something more. Much more.

A part of her was thinking, "This shouldn't be happening," while a louder part was saying, "Oh, shut up and enjoy the moment, for Pete's sake!"

Jake was kissing her, really kissing her, for the first time in her life.

She placed her hands on his shoulders and leaned closer. He wrapped his arms around her and pulled her onto his lap, his mouth hot and passionate. Yes-oh-yes-oh-yes. She wanted him so much and this time he wasn't shoving her away. She slid her fingers into his thick hair, wanting him to make love to her, to satisfy the onrush of desire building in her.

Ashley opened her mouth in silent invitation and he groaned as if in pain even as he accepted her offering. His marauding tongue teased her…exploring her lips, dueling with her tongue, igniting flames inside her.

She felt his arousal near her hip and knew he wanted her. Encouraged, Ashley slipped her hand down his chest, his stomach and abs, moving slowly until she reached the evidence of his desire. She sighed and laid her hand along the ridge behind his zipper.

With no warning, Jake jerked away from her, scooping her off his lap and back onto the sofa. He strode across the room and into the shadows near the window, his back to her. She could hear his harsh breathing and watched as he dropped his head to his chest, rubbing the back of his neck.

She covered her face, feeling as though he'd just dumped a bucket of ice over her. Like an idiot she'd let a kiss of gratitude go to her head, thinking he actually wanted her. Furiously, she dashed the unexpected tears away. She never cried. That wasn't who she was at all. Only Jake had the ability to reduce her to tears…and she hated her vulnerability where he was concerned.

She needed to go upstairs, to get away from him, to

exorcise from her brain what had just happened, but she was shaking too hard to risk standing right now.

Tremors coursed through her body, whether from the sudden onrush of desire the kiss had provoked or because of the humiliation she felt at the realization that once again she'd allowed herself to be captivated by Jake. She supposed it didn't matter why. All she knew was that she hurt.

She wrapped her arms around her waist and rocked, her eyes closed.

Ashley had no idea how long the room remained silent before Jake spoke. "I am so sorry, Ashley," he said gruffly. He cleared his throat. "I didn't mean that to happen. I, uh, I wouldn't blame you in the least if you left right now. My behavior was inexcusable."

She opened her eyes and saw that he'd walked back over to where she was. She took a couple of long, deep breaths and once she felt she was steady enough to speak, she replied, "There's no need for an apology, Jake. I'm the one who keeps offering my heart on a platter. Why blame yourself? This is a tough time for you…an emotional time." Forget about your flayed emotions, she told herself. They aren't his problem. Feeling calmer, she added, "I can understand what happened without reading anything into it."

When he remained silent, she said wryly, "You needn't worry about my reading something into an impulsive kiss. I learned and accepted a long time ago that you'll never be interested in me."

He sat on the edge of the chair across from her. His ferocious frown might have alarmed her if she'd had any energy left. "What are you talking about?"

"C'mon, Jake," she said, weariness settling deep within her. "The last time we kissed like that you treated me as though I had some kind of contagious disease."

He stared at her for a moment before speaking. "Are you talking about your birthday party?" He sounded puzzled.

"I'm sure you don't remember, but you completely humiliated me in front of your brothers that night." She took another deep breath. "Of course, I got over it eventually." A bolt of lightning should strike her for lying.

"I, uh, went looking for you that night to apologize, but I couldn't find you. After that, you never seemed to be around." He scrubbed his face with his hand. "I never, ever, meant to hurt you."

She nodded. "Probably not. However, I got your message loud and clear."

"I had no idea that you took my behavior that night to be a rejection of you." He shook his head in remorse. "Believe me, honey, it was anything but. You'd suddenly blossomed into a beautiful young woman and I was embarrassed that I reacted so strongly to you. You jolted me into seeing you as very desirable, which is why I had no business allowing this kiss to escalate tonight. I know how I react when you're around. I just wasn't thinking."

Puzzled by his explanation, she asked, "Are you saying you weren't repulsed by me that night?"

He raised his brow. "That's exactly what I'm saying. I'd never been turned on so fast in my life and it shocked me. I knew I had to stay away from you."

Ashley looked at him, trying to come to grips with this new revelation. If what he was saying was true, she'd completely misinterpreted his behavior that night. She'd caught him off guard and he hadn't known how to handle the situation.

A weight lifted from her, one she'd carried for much too long a time.

She wistfully smiled at him. "Thank you for telling

me that. It means more than I can possibly express." His expression eased a little. She wanted badly to throw her arms around him, but that would only make matters worse at the moment. "About tonight. I'm no longer a teenager, Jake."

His frown returned. "I'm well aware of that, Ashley. I've been fighting the attraction I've had for you for years. Tonight was a mistake. We both know that. I just want you to know that you have my word that I won't take advantage of you if you should decide to stay here with Heather and me."

"I don't need your assurances, Jake." She paused, gathering her thoughts. The subject was too important to ignore now that she was in possession of knowledge about his feelings toward her. Her heart raced at the possibilities that were opening up for her. "The thing is, Jake, I see no reason for us to ignore the feelings we have for each other at this point in our lives. I've never made an attempt to hide how I feel about you and now you're saying that you're attracted to me, as well, that you've been attracted to me since I was sixteen…oh…except for the small matter of your having married someone else a couple of years later." Oh, boy. Now comes the hard part. I've come this far, I can't stop now. After another deep breath, she said, " But you're no longer married, Jake. And I'm no longer a child."

He flinched. She couldn't believe it. What was wrong with him? Couldn't he see the possibilities for their future? Or was he more interested in an intimate relationship only, with no strings attached.

"I agree, Ashley. You're no longer a child. But you're still young. You've got your whole life ahead of you. I don't want to…" He stopped speaking as though at a loss for words.

Why was he denying them the opportunity to explore the possibilities they might have? She couldn't believe this man!

"What are you, old and broken? Come on, Jake. The last I heard, thirty-three doesn't put you in the senior citizen group."

"The gap between us is important, though," he went on doggedly. "I'm more experienced, more—"

"So what if I told you I slept with every college guy I dated for seven years? Would that make a difference in your thinking?"

He stared at her in shock. "You did *what?*"

She was having trouble keeping a straight face, but she gave it her best shot. "Well," she said in her most reasonable voice, "if it's just a matter of who has more experience…." She shrugged her shoulders slightly and left the comment unfinished.

He blanched beneath his tan and it was only then that she realized he'd actually thought she was serious. "Oh for Pete's sake, Jake! I'm kidding. You know me better than that." Feeling stronger now that they were actually discussing their relationship, she stood. At least she'd given him food for thought. "As for my staying here to be with Heather for a while longer, let me sleep on it and I'll let you know my decision tomorrow."

He stood as well while she finished her remarks by saying, "As far as the relationship you and I have…you have the right to feel anyway you want where I'm concerned. It might help you come to terms with the idea of our spending time together if you dismiss the age difference between us that no longer matters, forget about the little girl you watched grow up and take a look at who I am today."

Jake rubbed a hand over his face and she saw how exhausted he was. "The thing is," he said wearily, "I'm not cut out to be a husband. I learned that the hard way.

If I were to attempt to have a relationship with you, I know I'd lose control and end up making love to you. I don't want to use you that way. You deserve a man without so much baggage. Right now, I feel considerably older than thirty-three, believe me." He raised his hand as though to touch her cheek, then dropped it. "I never ever want to hurt you, Ashley. I'm sorry that my clumsiness when you were a teenager gave you grief. That was the last thing I wanted."

"So what you're saying is that I need to forget about my feelings for you."

His ears turned red. Doggedly, he said, "I'm just saying that a relationship between us would be wrong for you."

She eyed him thoughtfully for a moment. "Tell you what. You let me worry about what's right or wrong for me, okay? You've made it clear I have no place in your life and I accept that. For now."

She turned and walked away from him.

"Ashley," Jake said, following her from the room. "I'm sorry. I know I'm not good with words and I don't explain myself well. I apologize if I offended you."

She paused at the bottom of the staircase and turned to him. "Oh, you haven't offended me, Jake. You've just made me question my sanity and my lack of intelligence for still being in love with you after all these years."

# Eight

Ashley absently closed the door to her bedroom, going over what had been said just now.

She'd misinterpreted his actions all those years ago. He'd admitted that he was attracted to her.

That said, she knew he still carried a torch for Tiffany. How could he not? Jake loved her when he married her and he was very loyal to those he loved. Hearing that she was on her way to get married again must have been painful. Added to that pain was his discovery that he had a daughter and Tiffany hadn't told him.

No wonder he was still reeling.

She understood that he was vulnerable; otherwise he wouldn't have admitted that he was attracted to her. She also knew that Jake had no intention of acting on that attraction, but his reasons puzzled her.

Why did he consider himself poor husband material? Why did he blame himself for Tiffany deciding to leave?

How could he believe that marriage wasn't for him? Maybe nothing would work out for the two of them in the long run, but couldn't he at least give their relationship a chance?

He was being as honest with her as he could be, she knew. He'd always been an honorable man. She was one of the few people who saw beneath his strong, taciturn surface to his kind and gentle heart.

Of course he didn't want to hurt her.

However, she knew that if she decided to stay here to be with Heather until he found someone permanently, there was a strong chance that despite his best intentions she and Jake would end up in bed together—considering the sparks that flew whenever they were around each other. The electricity created could light up New Eden.

Ashley had to be honest with herself. She could very easily end up with her heart broken—again—unless she accepted the reality of her situation.

Whether the decision was reasonable or not, Jake had no intention of getting married again. They might become sexually involved, but an affair was the most she could expect from him. Her childhood dreams about him were just that—from her childhood—and had no bearing on any choices she made now.

Her problem was that she'd wanted Jake Crenshaw from the time she understood what all those hormonal changes meant. Unfortunately, the past twenty-four hours had taught her that those feelings hadn't died away. Her life had turned into something magical and exciting since he'd come back into it, and that was without including Heather in the equation. She had definitely lost her heart to that little girl.

Before going to bed, Ashley checked on Heather. She smiled to find her sound asleep, covers in disarray.

Who wouldn't love this little chatterbox with the insatiable curiosity and outrageous remarks guaranteed to cause an adult to cringe with embarrassment?

Once in bed, Ashley was almost asleep when she remembered that she didn't have clean clothes to wear for tomorrow. She'd need to go to her dad's first thing in the morning and see what she might have left to wear at his place.

When Ashley opened her eyes the next morning, she found a pink rabbit in her face. She lifted her head and saw Heather lying on the other side of the rabbit, quietly humming to herself.

"Good morning, sunshine," Ashley said, feeling as if she'd been up most of the night. She felt more tired this morning than she had when she went to bed.

She pushed herself into a sitting position. "I didn't hear you come in. Why didn't you wake me up?"

Heather replied, "Mommy gets mad when I wake her up."

Ashley hugged her. "Well, I don't mind." She brushed blond curls away from Heather's face. "I bet you're starving, aren't you?"

She nodded vigorously. "Where's my daddy?"

"I don't know. Did you look in his bedroom?"

Heather nodded vigorously. "His covers were hanging off his bed, but he wasn't there."

"Maybe he's in the kitchen."

"Uh-uh. I looked. Maybe he's gone outside somewhere. After breakfast can I go outside?"

Ashley smiled and stroked Heather's cheek. "Do you want to look for your daddy?"

Heather dropped her gaze and nodded her head. "'Cause he might take me for a ride on a pony."

"Well, I guess you'll have to ask him the next time you see him. Why don't you wait while I get showered and dressed, then we'll get you dressed and make some breakfast? How does that sound?"

"Pancakes?" Heather asked hopefully.

"Sounds like a plan." Ashley bent and kissed Heather on the forehead. Before she could straighten, Heather hugged her around the neck and kissed her cheek. "I like you, Ashley. I hope you stay with me all the time."

"Well, we don't have to decide all of that now." She picked up her clothes from the day before and went in to take her shower. She wondered what kind of mood Jake was in this morning

There was no telling.

Once dressed, Ashley returned to find Heather on her own bed, playing with her plush animal friends. They settled on what Heather would wear, with Heather giving Ashley pointers on coordinating colors.

When they went downstairs they found the kitchen empty and most of a pot of coffee gone. She knew Jake got up early and tried not to read anything into the fact that he wasn't there. After all, he had no reason to see how Heather reacted this morning. However, there was a niggling thought at the back of her mind that suggested he might not be too eager to see her.

Since she'd finally decided to accept his offer of staying there nights, she guessed he'd have to live with her presence.

For Heather's sake, of course.

By the time Ashley had pancakes ready and a second pot of coffee waiting, she heard Jake's footsteps on the patio. He seemed to have built-in radar where food was concerned.

He walked into the kitchen and his eyes immediately sought out Ashley. The tension in him was palpable and the look in his eyes seared her with its intensity. She couldn't control the heat that immediately spread through her in response. Oh, boy, what a way to get your motor running first thing in the morning!

"Mornin'," he said with a brief nod. He went immediately to the coffeepot and filled his cup. Glancing at her out of the corner of his eye, he asked, "Did you sleep okay?"

"Yes. And you?"

"I slept just fine," he said through clenched teeth.

"I slept fine, too," Heather said, already at the table eating. "And look!" she said to Jake with a grin. "Pancakes!"

Ashley had made silver-dollar-size pancakes for her and she'd been eating them like they were ambrosia. Heather glanced at Jake hopefully. "Once I eat my brea'fast, could we go for a ride on a pony?"

Jake looked at his daughter and chuckled, his expression lightening somewhat. "I'm glad to hear you slept fine, too, and I think we might be able to work in a horse ride for you this morning."

Ashley placed three glasses of orange juice on the table and added coffee to Jake's cup. He sat down and sniffed appreciatively. "They sure smell good," he said. "Hope you didn't eat them all up before I got here."

Heather giggled. "Ashley made a whole bunch, see?" She pointed to the platter that Ashley set before them. Heather's mouth was dappled with syrup. She took a drink of milk before saying, "She's a good cooker, isn't she?"

Each of them looked at her in surprise. This was the first time she'd shown so much pleasure since she'd been there.

Ashley could see the emotion Jake fought to cover. "Yes, she is," he finally replied.

She sat next to Heather again and across from Jake. She admired how yummy he looked in the morning, freshly shaved. The cotton shirt he wore, its sleeves rolled above his elbows, emphasized his muscular arms and shoulders.

She made herself focus on her meal and the two of them ate in silence while Heather entertained them. She gave Jake a highly imaginative description of everything she'd seen yesterday while she'd been with Ashley, waving her fork in the air to punctuate some of her remarks.

Once they were finished, Ashley cleared the table while Heather watched Jake expectantly. "Is it time to go riding now?"

He stood and held out his hand. "Let's get some of that syrup off your face and hands and we'll go outside and look for a horse."

She slid out of her chair and hesitantly walked to him. Ashley watched Heather shyly slip her tiny hand into his. Heather looked up at him, her head bent back. "You're really big up close."

Jake went down on his haunches. "Would you like me to carry you so you can see everything from up here?"

She nodded and allowed him to wash her face and hands before she wrapped her arms around his neck and said, "Let's go."

Jake looked at Ashley and gave her a slow smile. Relieved that Heather was being a little friendlier to her father this morning, Ashley walked over to them and kissed each one on the cheek.

The look he gave her weakened her knees. Darn it, why did she have to blush right then, causing his mouth to tilt into a slight smile.

"Thank you for breakfast, Ashley. I enjoyed it."

"Me, too," Heather parroted. "I enjoyed it, too."

"It was my pleasure." She looked into his eyes. "By the way, I believe I'll take you up on the offer you made last night."

He eyed her warily. "What offer?"

"Why, to spend my nights here for now." She batted her lashes. "What did you think I meant?"

"Oh. Good. I think."

She laughed. "You cowboys go out and ride the range or something and I'll see you later."

"I'm not a boy!" Heather said indignantly.

"Of course you aren't. I should have said cowgirl."

Heather grinned at her, pleased with the correction.

Once again electricity seemed to bounce back and forth between Ashley and Jake. This was certainly going to be an interesting visit.

After they had gone outside, Ashley stood by the sink, her hands clasped beneath her chin, and watched as Jake pointed out to Heather all the different buildings and equipment around the ranch.

They were so beautiful together. She blinked furiously, not willing to give in to the emotions threatening to engulf her. She would enjoy spending time with them, she knew. It was getting used to being without them in her life that would be the hardest adjustment.

# Nine

"This is a big place," Heather announced from above Jake's head. They stood in the ranch yard while he tried to decide where to take her first.

The idea of placing her on his shoulders wasn't one of his better ones. He felt naked outdoors without his hat on but there was no way he could wear it while she had a death grip on his hair. He had one hand holding her steady and the other holding his hat.

"You know what we forgot?"

"What?" she asked.

"We forgot to get you a hat. If you're going to ride a horse, you need one."

"Like yours?"

"If I can find one. We'll go look in the barn."

She swung her legs again his chest.

"Ow," he said. "That hurts."

"Oh. Sorry."

As soon as they reached the barn, he swung her over his head and placed her on her feet, making her giggle. "You're strong."

"Sometimes, maybe. I've gotta admit you're heavy." She grinned. "'Cause I eat so much, right?"

"And because you're getting to be a big girl." He headed to the tack room to see if there was anything he could place on her head to shade her fair skin.

"Oooh," she said and he realized that she'd stopped. He turned around. Heather had discovered Jordan's horses. "Look at the ponies," she whispered. "They're really big, aren't they?"

"I doubt that Jordan would appreciate your referring to his thoroughbreds as ponies, but you're right, they're big."

"Can I ride one of them?"

He held out his hand and she took it as naturally as if she were used to doing so. "Well, we'll find one to ride, but not from this group." He let her walk into the tack room ahead of him. She was fascinated by the saddles, bridles, curry combs and other items needed around horses.

He spotted a small hat on one of the hooks. Probably belonged to one of the kids on the ranch. He sat it on her head, then knelt to see if it fit. It was a little big but better than nothing. He'd have to take her into town and get her some clothes that could stand up to ranch life.

The hat slipped over one of her eyes and she giggled. "I can't see."

He grinned and straightened it. "There. You'll have to hang on to it, though, or it's going to fall off."

"Howdy, you two," Jordan said, walking toward them. "How's everything going?"

Heather grabbed Jake's hand and leaned against his leg. "Who's that?" she whispered.

"This is my cousin, Jordan Crenshaw. Jordan, please

meet Heather Anne Crenshaw, who has taken up permanent residence with us."

Jordan raised his brows. "Well. How about that? I'm pleased to meet you, Miss Heather." He held out his hand.

She eyed it uncertainly, looked at Jake and then seemed to remember something. "These are your ponies, aren't they!" She took his hand briefly, then leaned against Jake again.

Jake cleared his throat, trying not to laugh at the expression on Jordan's face.

"Oh, well, yeah, I guess so."

"Do you get to ride all of them?"

He walked over to a bale of hay and sat down, which Jake thought was a good idea. He led Heather to another one nearby where they could be more at Heather's level.

"Not all of them, no. But I ride some of them."

She edged closer to Jordan. "He's going to take me riding on a pony."

"He? Don't you call him Daddy?"

She dropped her head and shook it slowly.

"We haven't gotten around to that, quite yet," Jake said easily. "It'll come."

"Well, you can call me Uncle Jordan, if you like. How about it?"

"Unca Jordan. Okay." She looked at Jake and he saw the flash of mischief in her face before she added, "And I'll call *him* Papa Jake!"

Jordan laughed and Jake joined in, shaking his head ruefully. "She's a character," Jake said, "I've already discovered that."

"Mommie calls me a pest sometimes," she nonchalantly shared with them. "Is that like a char—a chara—" She stopped, obviously frustrated. "I can't say it," she said, disgustedly.

Jordan picked her up, hugged her and set her back on

her feet. "You're a darling, is what you are. How come your daddy got so lucky, getting a little girl like you?"

Jake swallowed a couple of times in an effort to get the lump out of his throat. He needed to change the subject fast or his daughter was going to wonder what was wrong with him.

"Jordan, tell Heather about the time one of your horses jumped the fence and took off, why don't you?"

While Jordan described the incident, Heather came to Jake and held up her arms for him to pick her up. She settled onto his lap, rested her head on his chest and listened to the story about trying to catch a horse that didn't want to be caught.

Jake leaned down and softly kissed the top of her head.

Since April didn't work on Sundays, Ashley cleaned the kitchen and made up the beds. Afterwards, she went outside, wondering where her favorite Crenshaws might be.

She spotted them as soon as she stepped inside the barn. They were looking at a few of Jordan's horses. Jordan, who looked enough like Jake to be his brother rather than cousin, was talking to Heather, who appeared completely relaxed with the two men, which was an excellent sign that she was adjusting to her new situation.

Ashley stood there watching them. Chemistry was a strange thing, she thought, studying the two men. Jordan had the same Crenshaw stamp on him as Jake, so why was it only Jake Crenshaw who started her body humming?

Giving her head a quick shake, she called out to them. "I'm going to Dad's. Do you want to come with me, Heather?"

Both men turned at the sound of her voice, their brief smiles of greeting another similarity between them, their gleaming white teeth flashing in their darkly tanned faces.

Heather scrunched her face up—obviously in deep thought—and then shook her head. "I wanna stay with Papa Jake and Unca Jordan."

Papa Jake. So she'd found a name she was comfortable calling her father and uncle was as good a title for Jordan as any. Better than Cousin Jordan.

She waved and said, "See you later, then. Have fun."

Ashley took her time on the drive to her dad's place. She spotted deer grazing in one of the meadows and a red-tailed hawk watching for prey from the top of a utility pole. She loved this place and she didn't come out nearly often enough. Other than looking at Jordan's stock whenever he needed her, or checking on sheep or cattle that her dad called her about, she was rarely there.

She pulled up at Ken's house and parked beneath one of the cottonwood trees. Several large trees shaded the house, keeping the sun off the metal roof for most of the day. His truck was in the carport, so she knew he was home. She was looking forward to spending some time with him.

Her dad sat in his favorite easy chair, reading the Sunday paper and sipping on a cup of coffee.

"Hi, Dad," she said and smiled broadly.

He lowered the paper and looked at her with pleased surprise. "Well, hello, there, young-un," he said, getting up and giving her a bear hug that lifted her off her feet. "What brings you out here this fine summer morning? Not that I'm complaining, you understand."

"Jake probably told you about my keeping his daughter yesterday."

He nodded and motioned for her to precede him into the kitchen. "Yes, he did. Between worrying about Red, comforting his wife and feeling guilty that he hadn't gotten his daughter from you as planned, he was a bundle of nerves the entire day."

She poured herself a cup of coffee, filled his cup and sat at the kitchen table. Ken followed her, prepared to sit and chat. They'd spent many hours around this table over the years. Her dad had been a wonderful father and she counted herself very lucky. She had a parent who loved her unconditionally. She'd discovered while she was away at college how rare that was and how much she had to be grateful for.

She forced her mind back to the subject at hand.

"Well, as it turned out, Heather didn't want me to leave her once Jake got home, so I ended up staying over again. Rather than drive into town this morning for more clothes I thought I'd check my closet to see if I can find something I've left here."

He studied her, concern wrinkling his brow. "So you've spent two nights at Jake's," he finally said.

"That's right, Dad. Jake asked me last night if I would be willing to stay out here with Heather nights until he hires someone to look after her. I really don't mind the drive for a week or so. I fully expect him to find someone suitable by then."

Ken leaned on his crossed arms. "Do you think that's wise, honey?"

They both knew what he was concerned about.

"You mean because of that crush I used to have on him?" She chuckled. "Oh, I'm well over that by now." Of course you are, the voice in her head said with a sneer. You're crazy in love with him and you know it.

She cleared her throat. "Jake and I have been friends my entire life. I see no reason why I shouldn't help out a friend when he needs it."

"Maybe I'm behind the times, but two unmarried people of the opposite sex living together can cause a lot of grief for everyone concerned, friends or no friends."

"It's a big house, Dad. My time will be spent with Heather, not Jake. She trusts me and I don't want to let her down."

"Could this newly formed attachment you have with Heather have anything to do with her being Jake's daughter?" Ken asked with a lopsided smile.

She squeezed his forearm and smiled. "Probably," she admitted, "but she's really adorable. Once you meet her, you'll see what a little darling she is."

He covered her hand with his. "I just don't want to see you hurt, sweetheart. You've gone through enough grief in your young life."

"I know, Dad," she said softly.

"You're old enough to make your own decisions. I know that. And I think the world of Jake. Always have. I watched those boys grow up and I know the values they were taught.

"Jake is an honorable man, but his world has changed drastically and he's still reeling. He's vulnerable right now. As far as that goes, he's always been vulnerable where you're concerned. He's a man with strong emotions. The combination of his state of mind and your living there with him could be more than he can handle right now."

Ashley valued her dad's opinion because he knew Jake almost as well as he knew her. "Are you saying my being there will only make things worse for him? I want to make things a little easier for him."

Her dad had pointed out all the thoughts that had run through her head last night. Yes, Jake was vulnerable. Well, so was she.

"You have to do what you think best, sweetheart. I guess I'm concerned about the possible fallout. He's always had a soft spot for you."

She cocked her head. "I can't tell who you're most protective of, Dad, me or Jake."

"Both!" he immediately replied and they both laughed.

"Guess I'll go see what I can find to wear," she said after draining her cup. "While I'm here on the ranch, you'll be seeing more of me, you know."

"I'll hold you to that, young-un," he replied, patting her shoulder.

"I love you, Dad."

"Right back at you, sweetheart."

It was almost noon by the time she returned to Jake's place. She saw him on one of his horses with a tow-headed little girl in front of him, wearing a hat that she could barely peer out from under. She smiled at the picture they made. He must find it natural to have a little girl once again clamoring for a ride with him.

When Ashley got out of her truck, Heather waved at her and yelled, "Look at me, look at me, Ashley! I'm riding!"

Ashley waved back. "Good for you, sunshine." She drew closer and looked up at Jake. "You two get washed up and I'll see what's on hand to feed us."

"Good idea," Jake replied, looking relieved. "This gal has plumb worn me out."

"I can relate, believe me. I'll have something prepared by the time you finish your ride." She hurried into the house, not wanting to betray to him how touched she was by the sight of his big hand gently holding Heather close to his chest, keeping her safe.

When the riders walked into the kitchen, Ashley had soup and sandwiches waiting. By the time Heather finished her meal, she was almost asleep, her head nodding and her lashes drooping.

Jake came around the table and quietly picked her up. Ashley followed as he carried Heather upstairs to her room. After stopping in her room, she waited in the hallway, smiling. After a couple of minutes, he rushed out of the room, looking panicked. "Have you seen her—" He stopped when he saw Ashley holding the pink rabbit out to him.

"She left it in my room this morning."

"Thanks," he said, his relief obvious. He disappeared into Heather's room again and Ashley heard Heather's sleepy murmur and his deeper voice, barely audible.

When he came out, she joined him companionably as they walked downstairs.

Ashley stopped in the hallway and said, "You know, I think that while she's asleep, I'll go into town and pack some things. I won't need much, since I'll be stopping by my apartment each day to check my mail. That is, if you don't mind being here alone with her."

"I really hate to ask you to do this. I know you've got better things to do with your time than to hang around here."

"I wouldn't be doing it if I didn't want to. I had a choice, you know. Nobody forced me." She smiled. "Don't worry so much, Jake," she said. "Let's take this one day at a time."

"It's not the days I'm worried about," he replied darkly.

"Really? Well, maybe you should be," she said, and went up on tiptoe to kiss him.

Jake froze when her lips touched his and she thought he was going to push her away. Instead, he took over the kiss.

How quickly she'd become addicted to his touch. She loved the feel of his hands on her back, the muscled hardness of his chest. Oh, yes, this was what she needed.

When he finally released her, they were both breathing hard.

"You're not helping, you know," he said, his voice raspy.

She widened her eyes. "I'm not? I thought I took part in that kiss, but if I didn't, here, let me try again."

He stepped back, shaking his head and chuckling. "That's not what I meant and you know that very well."

"Jake? I see no reason why we can't enjoy being together and enjoying each other's company. Why are you fighting this?"

They hadn't moved away from the bottom of the stairs. She leaned against the newel post and looked at him.

"You're not that naïve, Ashley. This isn't about stealing a couple of kisses now and then. I told you how I felt about you last night. Now you're using my remarks against me."

"I'm not asking for anything from you that you aren't willing to give. If our making love will ease the tension between us—and we both acknowledge that it's what we want—what harm can it be?"

"Maybe you're used to casual affairs, but I'm not. I will not allow myself to get involved with you when there's no future in it."

She looked at him in silence before she finally said, "You're really angry at me, aren't you?"

He let out a gust of air and dropped his head. "Not really. I just don't want you to tease me when you know I have no intention of following up. We need some boundaries if you're going to stay here."

She folded her arms across her chest. "I see. So I'm making matters worse by showing my affection for you."

He turned away. "It's bad enough as it is, Ashley. I can't sleep at night, knowing you're down the hall from me, and if I do manage to sleep, I dream of you," he said, pacing.

"That pretty well describes my nights, too," she said softly.

He flinched. "I could have gone all day without knowing that, but at least you're being honest."

"I've always been honest, Jake. That's never been the issue. You seem to have some knight-like attitude toward me, treating me as your lady fair who can't be sullied by your base desires."

He glanced at her from beneath his brows and smiled sheepishly. "That bad, huh?"

"I'm not going to beg you, Jake. If you feel that your conscience won't allow physical intimacy between us, I can accept that. However, I'd appreciate your hiring someone as quickly as possible so that I can get back to my life without you in it. I'm counting on the old adage, 'Out of sight, out of mind.'"

# Ten

$A$shley closed her apartment door behind her, dropping yesterday's mail on the table, and went to the refrigerator for a soft drink. Popping the top on the soda, she walked to the picture window in her living room and looked out at the traffic going by.

She tried to convince herself that she was relieved to be back in her own home without a chattering little girl and a man who drove her crazy, but by the time she finished her drink she gave up the pretense.

How ironic that for the next week or so, she would be living the life she'd always wanted—living with Jake and caring for his child. Perhaps she should have been more specific in her dreams.

At least he was no longer patting her on the head—metaphorically speaking—and treating her as a child. In a way, his present attitude was worse. Because he was physically attracted to her, he didn't want to be tempted by being affectionate toward her.

She went into the bedroom. In addition to gathering some clothes to wear, she also needed to adopt a new attitude toward the Crenshaw father and daughter. Despite her dad's concern, she wasn't using Heather as an excuse to be there. She wanted to ease the transition for Heather and she knew she could do that.

What she'd do from now on would be to ignore Jake as much as possible. And take sleeping pills at bedtime.

Heather was up from her nap when Ashley returned to the ranch. She could hear her in the kitchen. When she heard Jake laugh, she smiled at the sound and walked into the room.

Jake had found the Popsicles she'd bought yesterday and had given one to Heather, who seemed to be enjoying it immensely—if the strawberry-red color around her mouth and chin were any indication.

"Ashley! You're here. I missed you. I couldn't find you when I waked up."

"I promised you she would be back soon," Jake said, glancing in Ashley's general direction without meeting her eyes. He returned his gaze to Heather. "And here she is."

"I don't want you to leave me, Ashley," Heather scolded. "Not ever again."

Ashley poured herself a glass of water to give herself some time before she said, "Here's the deal, sunshine. I have to go to work every day and I can't take you with me most of the time. Sometimes, maybe, but not often. So you'll be with your daddy during the day and when I finish taking care of the animals who come see me, I'll come home and spend the evening with you."

"And the night," Heather added, sounding insistent.

"For a while, I'll stay the night, too."

"But I want you to always stay here."

Jake was conspicuously silent. Darn him, anyway.

"Won't happen, little girl. You'll have to take what you can get." She picked up her small duffel bag and said, "I'll put this upstairs and see what we can have for supper."

Matching her actions to her words, Ashley went upstairs. When she entered her bedroom, she closed the door and sank into a chair. Her suspicions about herself were confirmed.

She was a masochist.

The following Friday, Ashley ushered out the day's last patient and his owner and stood beside Wendy's desk until they were gone.

"I think that's it for my day. What does tomorrow look like?"

"Busy, as usual. At least you won't be on call this weekend."

"Thankfully. I'm counting the days until the newly graduated doctor of veterinary medicine joins us. Even with Woody and I working full-time, the practice has grown too much for the two of us to handle."

"It hasn't hurt that the two of you have lived here all your life. People trust you."

Ashley wriggled her shoulders and stretched. "That's good to know. At the moment, all I want to do is sink into a steaming bath for an hour and afterwards fall on the bed until morning."

"Sounds like a plan."

Ashley grinned. "With a three-year-old around? Not a chance."

"You haven't mentioned how things are going out there."

"Progress all around. Jake flew to Austin and San Antonio this week and interviewed applicants. He doesn't appear particularly thrilled with any of them, but they're qualified and interested to see the area. Two are scheduled to visit next week sometime. As for Heather...on the one hand, she and Jake are more relaxed around each other. I think she's beginning to develop a certain pleasure from living on the ranch."

"What's on the other hand?"

Ashley sighed. "She still insists she doesn't want me to move back to town. Since Jake hopes to have someone hired by the end of next week, Heather will have to accept that she can't have everything her own way."

"The community has taken quite an interest in the goings-on out at the ranch these days. The buzz that Jake has a child no one knew about has kept the phones hot. With you in the mix, the phones at my place are suddenly quite active as well."

"Too bad there's so little entertainment in town. I can't imagine why anyone cares."

Wendy grinned. "Aw, c'mon, Ashley. Here's the very sexy, very eligible bachelor and his little girl and the very sexy, very eligible veterinarian spending her leisure time with the two of them. That's fodder for any gossip mill and you know it."

"As my grandmother was fond of saying—if they're talking about me, they're leaving someone else alone. It won't be long before something new and scandalous will draw their attention away from us."

"Well, I keep telling those who call that there's absolutely nothing clandestine about this whole setup, but I'm not sure anyone's buying that."

"Too bad."

"If you don't mind my saying so, you're looking pretty tired these days. Maybe you need to schedule a day off."

"I'm okay. Just not sleeping too well."

"I see."

"And the raised eyebrows mean…what?"

"Oh, nothing."

"C'mon, Wendy. You have something to say. Say it."

Wendy straightened in her chair and with a hint of amusement in her eyes, said, "Just wondering if Jake has anything to do with your sleeplessness?"

"If you're suggesting that I'm sleeping with him, you're wrong."

"Ah."

"What does *that* mean?"

"It's possible that the reason you aren't sleeping well is because you're *not* sleeping with him."

Ashley laughed ruefully since she knew her comment was right on the mark, but she'd never tell Wendy that.

"You're incorrigible and I'm out of here. I may have you schedule a day off for me some time next week. We'll keep it in mind and hope that an epidemic doesn't strike any of our clients."

With a final wave, Ashley stepped out of the clinic and decided to go downtown for a few items she needed at the drugstore.

After she parked, Ashley paused a moment to look at the square. From the activity around the business area, every citizen of the community was out shopping today.

Several people spoke or waved to her as she walked to the corner drugstore. She passed one of her former classmates, who asked, "How's Jake?" with such arch meaning Ashley almost laughed out loud.

"Terrific," she replied, continuing into the store. Let her take that any way she pleases.

Once she was on her way to the ranch, Ashley seriously wondered if she could sneak into the house without Heather or Jake spotting her. If so, she might be able to have that long, soaking bath after all.

She and Jake had settled into a routine of sorts. Mostly he stayed out of her way, which was a relief. She spent her evenings with Heather until she went to sleep somewhere around eight o'clock…too early for Ashley to go to bed.

If it weren't for the tension between them, she'd have no problem going downstairs to see how Jake's day went. After the first evening, though, she learned to go to her room and read. He continued to watch her as though expecting her to pounce on him the minute he relaxed.

She sighed. Not that she could blame him, she supposed. She'd initiated the kiss last Sunday and his reaction taught her never to let her impulses get the better of her again.

One night this week, she'd gone to the kitchen for something to drink and saw the light on in his office. The door was closed. I get it, I get it, I'm intruding on your space and I'm sorry.

At least he'd not wasted any time looking for someone to care for Heather. She would be just as glad to return to her normal routine as he was so that she could once again sleep at night.

Jake and his men rode slowly back to the ranch settlement, men and animals exhausted.

The sheriff had called this morning to say that his investigations into the recent rash of car thefts in the area led him to believe that the perpetrators were hiding somewhere on Jake's property. Because of the size of the ranch, there were areas his crew seldom visited, especially the sections that were rough and hard to reach. He flew over these on a regular basis, but no one had actually ridden in for a thorough inspection in a while. If the thieves *were* hiding on the ranch, they must have chosen the most inaccessible places, which didn't make much sense. If that were true, how were they getting in there?

He had gotten the call after Ashley had already left for the clinic. When he explained the situation to Jordan and told him that he and some of his men needed to search the property by horseback, Jordan offered to keep Heather with him. Jordan told him he had to run to town anyway and then go to his place to see how the construction of his horse barn was going, so she wouldn't be a bother.

Jake knew that his daughter could talk the ear off a deaf person, but he needed help. He was reluctant to ask Ashley to do more than she was already doing.

He and his men spent the day looking for tracks and checking the canyons and ravines. Jake brought his map of the ranch and had the men spread out to cover as much ground as possible.

When he got home, Jake wearily unsaddled his horse, rubbed him down and gave him extra rations.

Jake wished he could have a rubdown, as well. His body was signaling that it was no longer used to long trail rides and that he was going to pay for it.

This was the time of day he dreaded the most, when he had to be around Ashley. He made it a point to leave the house before the others were awake, but there was no way to avoid evenings with her until after Heather went to bed. After that, he took the coward's way out and stayed in his office, catching up on his accounts and watching television until he was convinced he could sleep.

Hah! It didn't matter whether he spent time with Ashley or not, his subconscious reminded him of her every time he closed his eyes. As tired as he was, he'd probably pass out as soon as he hit the bed tonight.

Then he remembered that today was Friday and he'd promised his poker-playing pals a chance to win some of their money back.

Damn.

Well, there was no help for it. He had to go. A hot shower and something for his sore muscles would have to do him. At least he didn't have anything planned for the weekend. Maybe he'd take Heather somewhere and get her used to not having Ashley around.

Yeah. He could do that.

Since he hadn't seen Heather all day, he knew she'd be full of stories to tell him. That should get them through the evening until her bedtime. Then he'd head into town.

At least he had a plan of sorts.

Two of the applicants he'd decided were what he might be looking for—after screening at least a dozen or more—were willing to live here in the Hill Country and he'd arranged to fly them to the ranch next week. They were comfortably middle-aged and he hoped whoever he chose would remind Heather of her Gram and ease her away from wanting Ashley there every day.

He wasn't too sure that his thoughts and dreams of her would stop once she'd moved back to town, though.

A small voice in his head had been whispering repeatedly for the last few days, "Marry her."

He'd tried to ignore the thought, but the idea lodged in his brain and he couldn't get rid of it. The little voice refused to shut up. In fact, it built its case by pointing out the differences between his relationship with Tiffany and the kind he already had and could have with Ashley in the future.

He'd already faced the fact that he was in love with her. If he'd had any doubts, the past week had dispelled them. He knew every time he heard her voice and her laughter, every time he saw her, every time he wanted so badly to reach out to her and hold her as tightly as he could.

It wasn't that he doubted his love for her. It was the thought of being married again that gave him nightmares. Tiffany had put him through a great deal during their marriage, which was why he never doubted that she was capable of hiding the existence of his daughter from him.

That's when the voice would start in again.

Tiffany had never liked ranch life. Ashley had known no other. Tiffany spent thousands of dollars on clothes, makeup and keeping her hair and nails looking just right.

He'd rarely seen Ashley in anything but jeans and shirts and if Ashley used makeup at all, it was probably lipstick. She definitely had an easy-to-keep haircut that made her look adorable.

If he'd had any sense, he would have married Ashley in the first place—if she hadn't been so blasted young. "That was then. She's no longer a teenager," the voice slyly pointed out.

When he left the barn, Jake wondered where Jordan and Heather were. His errands should be finished by now. There was Ashley's truck. Maybe Jordan had already dropped Heather off and had gone home.

Once inside the house, he didn't hear a sound, which was pretty much a guarantee that Heather wasn't here, or if she were, she was asleep.

The answering machine was blinking and he punched the play button. The message was from Jordan. He could hear Heather chattering in the background as well as other voices.

"Hey, Jake," Jordan said, sounding amused. "Didn't want you to worry about us. I stopped by the folks' place to show our baby girl off and Mom invited us to stay and have dinner with them tonight. They want to get to know Heather and I didn't think you'd mind. I'll have her home by dark."

Since it was already seven, Jake figured they would be back no later than eight, which would be close to Heather's bedtime and time for him to go to town.

He wondered where Ashley was. She was usually in the kitchen when he came inside. Jake took the stairs two at a time and paused in front of her door. He knocked gently. If she was asleep, he didn't want to disturb her. When there was no answer, he quietly opened the door to make certain she was there, but her bed was untouched.

As he turned to leave he noticed the light on in her bathroom and the door open. "Ashley?" he said and waited for an answer. When none came, he became more alarmed. Was she ill?

He stopped in the doorway of the bathroom and saw her reflected in the mirrored wall. She was in the tub sound asleep. His brain immediately shut down. He stood there frozen as though in suspended animation. He knew he had to leave…he really had to. Seeing her like this was the absolute last thing either one of them needed.

But what if she drowns? It was dangerous for her to sleep in the tub like that.

Jake slowly stepped into the room, trying to figure out a way to wake her without startling her.

She must have been covered by frothy bubbles at one time but now the water was clear except for a few clumps of foam that formed little islands on the surface. The pink tips of her breasts rose slightly above the water.

No longer capable of rational thought, he knelt beside the tub.

She had an air pillow at her neck, cushioning her

head from the porcelain surface. Soft music played from a nearby radio. She looked so relaxed that he suddenly realized how strained she'd looked all week, pretty much the way he looked in the mirror each time he shaved.

Now her face was softened by sleep, her body floating in full view.

There was no doubt in his mind that he'd just lost the struggle to leave her alone. He knelt beside the tub, drinking in her beauty. Her breasts were in proportion to her small build; her waist dipped in and her hips flared in perfect symmetry; her flat stomach and legs were muscled and firm without losing the delicate look that was Ashley.

He closed his eyes, but it didn't help. She was now imprinted on his brain permanently. When he opened them, he said her name like a prayer.

"Ashley," he whispered, hurting inside.

Her thick lashes fluttered and she opened her eyes.

# Eleven

**A**shley was dreaming of Jake. She wasn't surprised to hear him softly call her name. She opened her eyes and knew that this was no dream. She must have fallen asleep and Jake now knelt beside the tub.

He looked hot, tired and dusty. There was a line across his forehead where his hat had rested. The rest of his face looked like he'd been in the sun most of the day.

Despite his obvious weariness, he wanted her and he made no effort to hide it. Belatedly, she became more fully awake and realized that there must be something wrong for him to be in her bathroom.

"Are you all right?" she asked, sitting up in the tub. When she realized the bubbles no longer covered her, she automatically covered her breasts with her hands.

"Don't," he whispered, as though pleading. He gently lifted her hands away. "You are so beautiful and I want you so badly I ache with it." His voice died away as he trailed his fingers through the water and cupped her breast. His soft touch made her intensely aware of her overwhelming need for him.

She reached for him and he pulled away. "I'm filthy," Jake said. "I have no business in here. It's just…"

She nodded to the glass shower next to the tub. "There's plenty of soap and water right here." She flushed as she added lightly, "I'll be glad to help you bathe."

If that didn't make her feelings for him clear, then nothing would.

As though in a trance, Jake sat on the commode and pulled off his boots and the rest of his clothes. He stood and turned on the shower.

Oh, my, not even her wildest imaginings had done justice to his beautiful, unclothed body. His wide shoulders and muscled back tapered to his waist and down to his firm butt.

He could have posed for Michelangelo with his pure, clean lines and strong, healthy body. She wanted to touch him so badly, needed to love him so much, that she quivered with yearning.

She watched him step into the shower, pick up the soap and begin to lather himself. As though caught in his force field and unable to escape, she slowly stood and silently stepped over the side of the tub. He had his back to her and when the door opened behind him he looked around, startled.

"Here," she said, taking the soap from his hand, "let me."

Without a word, he gave her the soap and turned back to the wall, leaning with his palms against the tile in surrender.

Ashley indulged herself in all the ways she'd dreamed about. She stroked and caressed his shoulders and back with soapy hands, her fingers trailing over him. She took special care to massage his hard backside and noticed his legs had a tremor in them.

When she tugged on his arm he slowly straightened and turned, revealing his arousal, his arms at his sides. He'd closed his eyes and stood before her without moving. She realized that he'd finally surrendered to the inevitable passion between them.

She soaped his shoulders, arms and chest, luxuriating in the freedom to touch him to her heart's content.

He remained still and silent until she carefully washed his groin area, running her fingers down his aroused length and cupping him. He groaned as though in agony and opened his eyes.

"I can't resist you," he whispered brokenly. "No matter how hard I try. I want you so damned much!" He lifted her breasts in the palms of his hands and bent over to kiss them, the spray of water sluicing the soap she'd applied off him.

When his mouth surrounded the tip of her breast, she went up on her tiptoes in encouragement while she restlessly stroked him, wanting him, eager to have him deep inside her.

He slipped his arms around her and lifted. She clung to him, wrapping her legs around his waist. He kissed her, turning so that her back was against the tile. As though a dam had broken inside of him, all his pent-up emotions swept over them and he devoured her, stroking her mouth with his tongue, nibbling on her bottom lip, his hand kneading her breast.

She could feel his arousal pushing lightly against her, ready to enter. Oh yes please oh please yes oh yessss. They were panting for breath as he shifted slightly and—

"Hey, Jake! Ashley? Anybody home?"

They froze and stared at each other in shock. Jake dropped his head back with a groan. "How could I have forgotten?" he muttered. He carefully lowered her to her feet. "It's Jordan, bringing Heather home." They were both shaking and Ashley wasn't certain she could stand without his help.

He braced her and said, "His timing couldn't have been worse."

She focused on the heated expression in his eyes. "Either that, or you were saved from breaking your rules by a metaphorical bell," she shakily replied.

"The rules never entered my mind, but we've got to get out of here before he comes upstairs looking for us."

Her brain must have been scrambled by lust. She quickly left the shower while he turned off the water. She threw him a towel while she quickly dried off. "I can't believe I totally forgot about her!" she whispered in panic.

"What about me? I knew they would be here soon and I still forgot!"

"Stay here. I'll get you some fresh clothes in a few minutes," she said in a low voice, pulling on underwear. She raised her voice and called out. "Just a minute, Jordan, I'll be right there."

Jake finished drying off and wrapped the towel around his waist. He quickly gathered up his dirty clothes. "I think they're on their way up here. If so, take them downstairs and I'll be able to get to my room."

Ashley slipped into a pullover shirt and jeans and left the bedroom barefooted. She found Jordan at the top of the staircase holding Heather. "Hi, Jordan!" she said brightly, hoping he couldn't read anything in her expression. "And Heather, you look like you're more than half asleep! Sorry I didn't hear you when you first got here." She motioned to her wet hair. "I was in the shower." She knew she looked flushed and hoped Jordan thought it was due to the hot water and not because she'd been with Jake.

Ashley led the way downstairs as she talked. "I thought Heather was with Jake. How come you have her?"

Jordan put her down and said, "Oh, he'll explain once he gets home. We had a great day, didn't we, sprout? Took her over to show her off to my folks. I think Heather has pretty well talked herself into silence—at least for today."

"Can you stay? I'll get something together to eat and—"

"We ate at Mom's and I need to be going."

"Ah."

"Tell Jake to call me when he gets in."

"I'll do that."

Without a word, Ashley scooped Heather up in her arms and they went upstairs. Heather was almost half-asleep as Ashley took a washcloth and bathed her face and hands, put her in her pajamas and slipped her into bed. She placed the pink rabbit in the curve of her arm, kissed her on the cheek and left.

She heard the radio softly playing in her bathroom. When she went in to turn it off, she saw the water still in the tub. She drained and cleaned the tub, then went in search of Jake.

When she tapped on his door, he gave a muffled answer.

Standing outside his closed door, she said, "Jordan said to call him when you get in."

"I will."

After a moment of indecision, she finally spoke again. "I'm going to make us something to eat."

"Don't bother. I need to go into town and I'll eat while I'm there."

Stunned that he could leave right now, she managed to say, "Oh. Okay."

Ashley turned and retraced her steps until she reached

the kitchen. Maybe he had enough experience in this kind of situation to ignore the body's screaming need for relief, but she didn't. She could scarcely stand still, so she paced and rubbed her arms, attempting to talk herself down from this new place she'd just discovered.

Sometime later, while she stood at the kitchen bar half-heartedly eating a sandwich, she heard him come down the stairs, cross the foyer without pausing and go out the door.

She had never been this sexually aroused before and had no idea what to do about her discomfort. She wasn't in pain, exactly, but her skin was sensitive and she was aware of the clothes she wore touching and rubbing against her. Her whole body felt hot and prickly.

Would a cold shower really help? Somehow—given the circumstances just before Jordan arrived—she didn't think so. After what had almost happened, she'd probably become aroused every time she walked into her bathroom.

She tried to watch television, but nothing appealed to her. She picked up and put down a couple of magazines and searched the shelves for a book to read, but nothing caught her eye.

Finally, she gave up and went to bed, lying awake for hours wondering where Jake had gone and why. Had he already planned a meeting in town when he found her in the tub? She still didn't know why Jordan had kept Heather. She and Jake hadn't done much talking.

She buried her head in her pillow and groaned.

Had he gone to another woman to take care of his needs? The thought really depressed her.

Ashley eventually fell asleep, her dreams filled with images of Jake.

Jake drove into town as though all of the demons in hell were after him. He knew he was a coward for not talking to Ashley before he left about what had happened. What could he have said? All his high-minded resolve to leave her alone went up in flames when he saw her asleep in the tub.

Should he admit how much he loved her and, because of those feelings, how little control he seemed to have where she was concerned?

Should he admit how painful it was to love her while knowing she deserved someone better than him? Explain why he didn't ask her to marry him?

When he arrived at the Mustang Bar & Grill, Jake still had no answers, only more questions.

When he went inside, most of his poker-playing buddies were already there, eating hamburgers. He motioned to the waitress to bring him the same and sat down with them.

"Hi," he said to the group.

Kent and Lew, the other ranchers, looked at each other before Kent asked, "Who died?"

The waitress brought his beer and he drank almost a third of it with his first swallow. Once she left, Jake said, "Nobody died that I know of. Why do you ask?"

Banker Tom laughed and said, "Well, you look like you at least lost your last friend, which can't be the case since we're all here." The other three laughed.

"Just tired. I've been on horseback all day and I'm here to tell you I much prefer a pickup. It's a hell of a lot more comfortable."

Lew nodded. "I hear you. That's why I hire men to do that sort of thing for me."

Jake told them why he'd been out searching the ranch and by the time he'd finished eating, the conversation had turned to more general matters.

They went into the back room and gathered around the table. Tom eyed him from over his glasses. "Hope you brought some of my money with you 'cause I intend to win it back tonight."

Jake forced a smile. "You can try."

He kept thinking about Ashley and what had almost happened today. He knew he wouldn't get the image of her in the shower with him out of his head.

"Your turn, Crenshaw," someone said, and Jake obligingly played.

As the night wore on, he knew his concentration was shot. He just couldn't get interested in the hand he had or the growing pot in the middle of the table.

Lew said, "I've been thinking about what the sheriff told you. Guess it could be worse. Instead of stealing cars, they could be rustling cattle."

Kent, who ran a large herd of longhorn cattle, said, "Mine are a little more difficult to crate and haul out of here, but you two running sheep and goats might have a problem."

"Well, gentlemen," Tom said genially, "while you've been discussing the perils of ranching, I just won the pot, or did anyone notice?"

The lawyer, Curtis, said, "Hell's bells, McCain, I've been paying attention. Didn't save me from losing my money any."

Jake yawned and tossed down his cards. "I think I'll head back home, guys. I'm exhausted and you've managed to wipe me out. I'll see you next week."

Once home, Jake paused in Ashley's doorway and watched her for a long time before he finally went to bed.

Jake kept himself as busy as possible during the next week. He and Heather had fallen into a routine of sorts since she'd arrived. She stayed with him mornings while he checked with Ken about what needed to be done that day and sometimes helped to supervise the work.

Around noon, he returned to the house where April had lunch waiting for them.

April had suggested during their first day on their own that she'd keep an eye on Heather while she napped, which would give him time to handle details without having to watch out for Heather. April would call him on his cell phone when Heather woke up and he'd swing by and pick her up, and then he would keep her with him until Ashley got home.

He asked Jordan's mother if she would watch Heather two afternoons that week while he flew to pick up each of the two applicants he considered qualified to be Heather's nanny. He didn't want his daughter to meet the applicants until he'd had a chance to evaluate them in his surroundings.

The first candidate gushed over everything she saw—the hacienda, the ranch buildings, the horses. She was so bubbly that he knew she would drive him crazy within a week…or sooner.

The second one, Charlotte James, seemed all right. She was calm with a gentle manner that reassured him she would be good with Heather. When he flew her back to the city, they discussed salary and when she might be able to come to work. They agreed that a thirty-day trial period would give them a chance to see if Heather took to her and if Mrs. James liked living so far from San Antonio. She told him she'd be able to start at the beginning of next week, which was fine with him.

Now that he'd found someone, he could rest easier. However, Jake knew that Heather wouldn't be happy about Charlotte's arrival if it meant that Ashley wouldn't be coming out to see her every day. She'd made that clear in a dozen different ways.

Heather was perfectly content to spend her days with

him, whether he was checking on things around the ranch, working on the books at home or running errands.

However, come evening, it was a whole new story. Ashley had worked late two nights this week and Heather had begun chanting "Where's Ashley?" as soon as the sun disappeared from the sky.

There were times when he felt like joining the coyotes baying at the moon. How had his life become so complicated in such a short time?

If Jordan hadn't shown up last week when he did, he would have been inside Ashley within seconds. Since then, he'd spent most of his evenings away from the ranch, leaving Heather to enjoy Ashley's company without his presence.

Ashley made no reference to what had happened. He'd wanted to apologize, but she seemed to be avoiding him as well and he could never catch her at a time when Heather wasn't there.

He'd had no business walking in on her like that and they both knew it. But it had happened. He'd long since forgotten about the little girl he used to know. His memories of seeing her in the tub and shower had shoved earlier memories of her out of his mind. The thought of attempting another marriage made him break out in a cold sweat. He didn't think he could survive another failure. However, he was beginning to think he didn't have a choice if he planned to protect her.

When Friday came, he was glad he had somewhere specific to go, rather than to continue driving the back roads listening to music on the radio until he felt safe in returning home.

He played a little better tonight and by the time they broke up, he was a little ahead.

It was midnight when he arrived at the house. He peeked in on Heather, who was blissfully asleep, straightened her covers and took a shower. He wasn't tired enough to guarantee that he'd immediately go to sleep, so rather than toss and turn, Jake decided to see what he could find in the refrigerator to eat. Maybe he'd watch a little television until he thought he could fall asleep. He'd spent way too many restless nights in bed to look forward to more of the same.

Ashley came awake, thinking she heard a noise. Her ear was attuned to Heather now and she wondered if Heather was having a bad dream. She didn't bother turning on a light before she went into Heather's room.

The little girl lay quietly sleeping. Ashley smiled. This child had two speeds—nonstop and sound asleep. Ashley was really going to miss her when she returned to her apartment.

Jake had mentioned, during one of his two-minute conversations with her this week, that he'd found someone suitable to stay with Heather. She would be coming to work on Monday.

She knew the announcement was his not-so-subtle way of letting her know she'd be leaving soon.

Thank goodness.

The tension in the house had grown worse this past week. They were like two magnets that immediately veered away from the other if they accidentally came too close.

The damage had already been done as far as she was concerned. Now she no longer had to imagine what Jake looked like nude and her dreams were much more erotic and explicit. Consequently, her sleep had suffered.

Once back in her room, she realized she was now wide awake. She decided to go downstairs for a glass of milk in hopes it would help her go back to sleep.

When she walked into the dark kitchen, she realized

that she *had* heard something. Jake, who stood in front of the open refrigerator gazing inside, must have made the noise.

His only apparel appeared to be jeans riding low on his hips.

As though sensing he was no longer alone, Jake turned and saw her. Silently he shut the refrigerator door, leaving the room lit only by the rays of the halogen light outside.

"I—uh—thought I'd get a glass of milk," she said, barely above a whisper.

He stood there in silence without moving.

How much more awkward could this be? He'd made it abundantly clear this past week that he had no intention of finishing what they had started in the shower. In fact, he'd acted as though it had never happened, which showed her how much he'd been affected by it.

She told herself to leave. She no longer wanted the milk. What she wanted to do was to disappear in a puff of smoke and be magically transported back to her bed. By morning, she would think of this as only a dream. A bad one, at that.

Ashley forced herself to take a step backwards but froze when he slowly moved toward her. He crossed the room in silence and stopped in front of her, then pulled her to him and held her, his face buried in her hair.

Her head rested on his chest and she could feel his heart racing. She hesitantly slipped her arms around his waist and stroked his bare back. He shivered and pulled her closer and she could feel his rigid length pressing against her.

"Ashley," he murmured as though in pain.

She tightened her hold and when he raised his head she looked up at him. "Yes."

They both knew what she meant and her softly spoken word seemed to release him from hidden restraints. He picked her up and strode to the living room directly across the foyer. He gently placed her on the sofa, unfastened his jeans so that they fell to his ankles, stepped out of them and knelt between her thighs.

Her short sleep shirt was no barrier as he eased it up to her waist. Then he waited, looking at her, although there wasn't enough light to see his face. She raised her arms and pulled him down where she could kiss him.

He caressed her, running his hands along her body until he reached her nest of curls. He teased her nipple with his tongue at the same time his fingers found the dampness between her legs.

Ashley exploded in a mind-blowing climax, bucking against him as she continued to keep her arms and legs around him.

His breath was ragged as he placed nipping kisses on her cheeks, along her jaw and her ears before blindly searching for her mouth. He pushed into her and paused.

"You're so small," he managed to get out. "I don't want to hurt you."

"If you stop now, *you'll* be in a world of hurts!" she whispered fiercely.

He made a sound of pained amusement. "I couldn't stop now if a train was bearing down on me." Matching actions to words, he pushed deeper inside her.

She tried not to flinch but she had to adjust to his size. He was huge. Of course, she had no experience in these matters but—

He eased up and began to pull away, but she tightened her hold around him with her arms and legs and forced his full length inside. This sensation was what she'd missed in the shower. If she'd only known, she might not have let him out of the shower, Jordan or no Jordan.

She knew when he discovered she was a virgin because he cursed beneath his breath, but he didn't stop. He kissed her, his tongue moving in rhythm to his movements. Her body clenched tightly around him and once again she went up in flames as she pulsated around him. He cried out and moved frantically inside her until he made one final lunge, holding still for a moment before he slumped against her, his weight absorbed by the cushions beneath them. His skin was damp everywhere they touched. She weakly ran her hands along his back, luxuriating in her ability to explore him at her own pace.

Her system continued in overload while her legs languidly slid along his hips and thighs and down to the sofa. They lay quietly for a few minutes before he began to withdraw from her.

"Don't!" she whispered, her arms reaching for him. He stood and yanked his jeans up, fastening them, and then picked her up and carried her to his room. After he closed the door behind him with his foot, he placed her on the bed and disappeared into his bathroom. When he returned, he placed a warm, wet washcloth between her legs, carefully touching her.

She should be embarrassed, she supposed, her mind lazily following what he was doing. But nothing Jake could do to her would make her shy.

When he crawled into bed with her, he pulled her over to him. She placed her palm on his chest, feeling the strong beat of his heart. When she leisurely slid her hand down his body she was surprised to discover that he was once again as hard as a rock.

"Jake?" she whispered.

"Go to sleep, love. I don't want you more sore than you already are."

She leaned over him and kissed him as seductively as she knew how. She slid her leg across him, straddling him, a position that placed him snugly against her. She pulled her sleep shirt over her head and tossed it aside.

"Ashley—" he said warningly but she had no intention of listening to him. Clumsily she reached down and guided him inside her, sighing with pleasure when he automatically lifted his hips against her.

She felt in control—gently rocking over him, kissing him, flicking her tongue against his coin-shaped nipples, and listening to his gasps of pleasure when she changed the angle or rhythm.

Although she wanted to keep her pace slow, her breathing quickened, the new and wonderful sensations building and building until she lost herself in them. Only then did Jake place his hands on her hips, picking up her rhythm and increasing it until they both exploded in a burst of heat and light, her sigh of satisfaction mingling with his.

When she could get her breath, she managed to say, "Wow."

He traced her spine with his fingers. "Yeah."

"I had no idea…" She didn't have the words to describe how she felt.

"Neither did I," he replied in a deep rumble.

She wanted to talk to him about what had happened and how it changed their relationship, but she was so relaxed that her mind wouldn't work.

She fell asleep on top of him and knew nothing more until she woke up in her own bed the next morning. She wondered at first if her dreams were getting more realistic until she moved and discovered that she *was* sore, just as Jake had predicted.

Ashley stretched and smiled. She had no intention of complaining. She was almost asleep again—neither one of them had gotten much sleep last night—when she heard a soft tap at the door. Could it be Jake? She hoped so.

"Come in," she said.

Heather peeked around the door.

"Good morning, sunshine. I guess you're ready for breakfast, aren't you?"

Heather shook her head. "Daddy fed me and told me he had some important errands to run and for me to stay with you today."

Ashley sat up and quickly held the sheet against her bare body. "Did he say how long he'd be gone?"

"Uh-uh, but he wrote something down and left it in the kitchen."

Her heart sank. Was he going to continue to avoid her despite what had happened last night?

Not if she could help it.

"Why don't you play in your room while I get my shower and dress, okay?"

"'Kay."

Fifteen minutes later Ashley walked into the kitchen. As Heather had told her, she saw a handwritten note lying on the breakfast bar. Oh, this was going to be good. She began to read.

*Sorry to leave Heather with you, but I have some errands to run and Heather wouldn't be happy trying to keep up with me. If you don't want to take her to your office this morning, Jordan said he'd watch her until you get home. I'll see you tonight and we'll sit down and discuss our relationship. Jake.*

"Why, Jake, honey," she said in a syrupy southern voice, "I swear, you do write the most romantic notes of anyone I know." In her natural voice, she added, "You rat."

"Who ya talking to, Ashley?" Heather said behind her.

"To myself," she replied. She turned and said,

"Would you like to stay with Uncle Jordan today while I go to work?"

"Why?"

"Why do I have to go to work?"

"Why can't I go to work with you?"

I'm going to kill that man as soon as I see him.

"Well, I'm going to be really busy today and I don't want you to get bored."

"Oh."

"But I'll be home in time to have lunch with you and we'll have the afternoon together. Won't that be fun?"

Heather smiled. "Uh-huh."

After she ate, Ashley took Heather outside to search for Jordan. He was never hard to find because he was generally with the horses. Sure enough, they found him in the barn.

As soon as she saw him, Ashley called, "Hey, Jordan, are you ready for a young visitor this morning?"

He'd been cleaning one of the horse's hooves when she called. He straightened and flashed his trademark Crenshaw smile. "You bet! Hi ya, Heather, I've got all kinds of fun things planned for us today." He winked at Ashley and said, "Try not to work too hard. We'll be here when you get back."

Ashley drove to town, still angry at Jake. Last night had been the most magical night of her life and she thought he'd felt the magic, as well.

So Jake wanted to talk about their relationship, did he? Well, she had a few things to discuss as well, such as his annoying habit of disappearing after making love to her.

What was his problem, anyway? Did he think she was going to insist that he make an honest woman of her? If so, she'd set his mind at ease. Chivalry certainly wasn't dead as far as Jake was concerned. No doubt he was somewhere rehearsing his speech about how he had taken advantage of her, and that what happened last night would not—could not—happen again.

Fine with her. Thank goodness Mrs. James would be here Monday and she could get on with her life without the stubborn man.

Jake could test the patience of a saint and she was certainly no saint!

# Twelve

Ashley and Heather were coloring in one of Heather's coloring books when Jake walked in around four o'clock.

"Hi, Daddy. Look what I'm coloring," Heather said by way of greeting. She held up her artwork.

Ashley had done her best to deal with the pain she felt at his disappearance today, but all it took was one look at him and the churning emotions she'd held in all day flooded over her.

He nodded at her without meeting her gaze and said to Heather, "What a pretty picture. I've never seen a green coyote before. I bet they're rare."

"Uh-huh, and guess what? Me and Unca Jordan went to this place where they have all kinds of games. You can throw balls and try to hit somep'n and then we went to this really noisy place and had hamburgers and—"

"Sweetheart, slow down and take a deep breath," Jake said, laughing and hugging her. "I'm glad you had a good time. I bet you were ready for your nap by the time you got home."

She nodded vigorously. "Ashley laid down with me and we both took a nap. She said she was really, really sleepy."

Jake flicked a glance at Ashley who sat at the table, her arms crossed. "So now you're awake and I bet more rested."

"Uh-huh, and you know what? I won a big dog at the game place!"

Jake started. "A dog? What kind of dog?"

"Wait here and I'll show you," Heather replied, racing out of the kitchen.

Jake went to the refrigerator and poured himself a large glass of iced tea. "Want some?" he asked, holding up the pitcher.

"No thanks."

He sat down across from her. "What kind of dog did she bring home?"

She looked at him and almost laughed at the apprehension in his face. "Don't worry. It's only a stuffed one."

"Whew! That's a relief." He drank some of his tea before speaking. "Did you sleep okay?" he asked, finally meeting her eyes.

"I must have, since I don't remember returning to my own bed last night."

He flushed and looked down at his tea. "I didn't think it would be a good idea for Heather to find us together."

"I agree."

Silence fell between them. Ashley could think of nothing to say that wouldn't include a comment about his leaving this morning.

The tension between them was so thick Ashley could almost see it.

Finally, he said, "I thought we'd wait until after her bedtime to talk about things."

"All right." She'd known this time would be coming soon. After all, Charlotte would be here in the next day or two. She needed to pack and go home, but not before she had to listen as Jake apologized profusely for what happened the night before.

She really didn't want to hear it.

Heather came skipping back in the room carrying a large stuffed dachshund by its middle, its body dangling on either side. "Here he is. Isn't he cute? I named him Ralph."

"Ralph?" Jake echoed. "Why Ralph?"

"'Cause I like that name."

"Then Ralph it is." He studied the stuffed animal a moment and added, "Ralph's certainly big."

Ashley watched him chat with his daughter, laughing at her stories, enjoying her presence. There were so many things that she loved about Jake, which was the reason she ached so. Why did she have to fall for this one particular man? There were a couple of men in town she had gone out with from time to time. They were better-looking than Jake, they were younger than Jake, but the problem for her was, they weren't Jake.

Well, she'd known when she agreed to stay out here that being around him would cause her more pain. Being fair, though, she knew that making love to him had been a healing of sorts for her. When she left, she'd have her memories of him as he'd been while making love to her, gentle and oh, so loving. Those memories would replace the unhappy ones she'd carried since her teens.

While she waited, she prepared herself for rejection yet another time.

Once Heather was in bed, Jake suggested they sit out on the patio. Ashley didn't mind because it was darker out there. She appreciated the fact that he didn't suggest the living room.

They took the pitcher of iced tea and ice-filled glasses with them and sat at the glass-topped table.

Once seated, Ashley waited to hear what he had to say…as if she didn't know. His first words surprised her.

"You're upset, aren't you?"

She frowned. "Why do you ask?"

"I've known you too long not to recognize most of your moods. Do you want to talk about it?"

She drew a deep breath. "All right," she said after a long pause. This was as good a place to start their conversation as any. "After both occasions when we made love, you disappeared. I more or less understood that you'd gone to your weekly poker game on Friday, so I waited for the chance to talk with you. You avoided me all week. Until last night. I woke up this morning and you were gone.

"I guess what's upset me is how you can be so warm and loving one moment and then pull your disappearing act the next. Last night was the most beautiful experience for me and I thought we'd reached a new understanding in our relationship. Apparently, I was wrong."

"I left before you woke up because I wanted to get back as soon as possible." He reached into his shirt pocket and pulled out something, placing it on his palm. "I flew to Dallas to get this for you."

Ashley stared at the ring in astonishment that he would purchase something so obviously expensive. Was this how he intended to repay her for helping with Heather? Surely he wasn't crude enough to offer it because they'd gone to bed together.

Was he?

"The ring's beautiful, Jake, but it really isn't necessary. I've enjoyed looking after Heather and there's no reason for you to—"

"I guess I'm not making myself very clear, here," he said, sounding nervous. "The ring is my rather awkward way of asking you to marry me."

"I don't understand. You've made it clear to everyone who knows you that you never intend to remarry." The shock of the ring and his proposal had her thoughts scattering. What was going on here? Jake Crenshaw proposing? Hadn't she dreamed of this very moment for years?

She looked at him for a long moment trying to read his expression, but he wasn't giving anything away. This must be his poker face.

"Why?"

He blinked, obviously startled by her unexpected question.

"Why do I want to marry you?" he carefully repeated, as though not sure he understood her question.

"Yes."

"Why does anyone propose marriage, Ashley? I thought this was what you wanted."

"Generally, a proposal is offered when there's love involved."

He looked offended. "Well, of course I love you and you've said you love me. I just thought that—"

"Is this about last night?"

He dropped his gaze. "Well, sure, that's part of it. But then there's Heather. She needs a positive mother figure in her life and since you've got to know her, I figured this will work out well for all of us."

"I see." She truly did. If he couldn't have Tiffany, he'd settle for convenience and she was already here. His feelings weren't so deeply involved that she could hurt him, even if she turned him down.

Was she going to turn him down?

At the moment, she was too confused to make a decision. There was a battle going on between her heart and her head. Her head pointed out what it would do to her, being in a marriage of convenience and the only one in love. Sure, he loved her. He'd loved her as a kid. This was more of the same, a symbolic pat on the head that said, "You've been a good girl, so I'll offer you your heart's desire and marry you."

Her heart kept saying, "At least you'd be with him and with Heather. You could have the family you always wanted, the one with little Jakes running everywhere…and a few little Ashleys as well."

Was it worth the price she'd have to pay?

"Ashley? Did you fall asleep?" He sounded half joking and half concerned.

"Oh, I'm awake, Jake. Finally." She leaned her forearms on the table and said, "What this proposal and its timing is all about is that we made love last night. Isn't that true?"

"Last night maybe rushed things along a little." His lips turned up in the corners. "Let's just say that I'm sorry our wedding night came before the proposal." He shrugged. "I guess it's obvious by now that I have no control where you're concerned."

"Tell me something, Jake."

"What?"

"Do you propose marriage to every woman you have sex with?"

He stared at her as if she'd slapped him.

"What kind of question is that?"

"One you might want to take a look at. You say you can't control your reactions to me and this is your way of having sex without guilt. Well, thank you for the offer," she said, her heart crumbling into aching pieces. "But I believe I'll pass."

He looked shocked. Guess he'd never been turned down before. She fought the tears that threatened. The last thing she wanted was for him to know how devastated she was by his reasons for proposing. The irony didn't escape her. Her youth had been filled with dreams of the time when he'd propose to her and now that he had, she'd refused him.

Finally, he said, "So what was last night all about, Ashley? You wanted a little fun in the sack and thought I'd be the one to experiment with? Is that all it was to you?"

"No! Of course not. It's just that I don't believe last night created a reason for us to get married." She handed him back the ring.

He stood. "I'm sorry that you find my proposal—and my ring—so offensive." He turned and went inside, quietly closing the door behind him.

She had to get away. Otherwise, she was going to make a blubbering fool of herself. As was the practice on the ranch, she'd left her keys in the truck. She hurried to her truck and drove to her dad's house.

He took one look at her face when she walked in, closed the door and held her. "Oh, Daddy, you were so right," she said, between sobs.

"I usually am," he said with exaggerated humility. "Exactly what have I been right about now?"

"I should never have moved in with Jake and Heather."

"Ah."

They stood there in the living room until she managed some semblance of control. He handed her his handkerchief in silence.

"I've been such a fool."

"Why do you say that?" He led her into the kitchen and poured her a glass of her favorite wine.

"Because it's true." She took a sip of wine, paused, and took another, larger drink. "This tastes so good. Thanks."

"Let's go sit in the living room and you can tell me what's happened."

They each sat in one of the overstuffed chairs facing each other. Ashley tried to gather her thoughts while she sipped the wine. The last thing she could tell her father was that she and Jake had made love. He'd call her all kinds of fool and she'd have to agree with him. How could something so beautiful turn out to be so painful?

She sighed. "He asked me to marry him," she said quietly.

"No kidding! Well, no wonder you're upset! Do you want me to give him a good talking-to for insulting you that way?"

She looked at him in disgust. "Not funny, Dad."

"Well, I think you could lighten up a little, don't you? I can't see why him asking you to marry him would upset you."

She swallowed. "Because it would be convenient for him to marry me. I'd be there for Heather, and for him." She stumbled over the last words.

Ken frowned and leaned forward, elbows on his knees. "What is it, sweetheart? Are you afraid of marital intimacy? I know I wasn't very good at explaining all that, and I'm sorry."

She rolled her eyes. "Oh, Dad, please. Every child living on a ranch knows all about the mating process and no, I'm not afraid of marital intimacy. I just don't want to have three people in the bed, that's all."

"Three!" He stiffened. "Are you telling me that Jake actually—"

"I'm talking about the ghost of Tiffany, the woman

he loves but no longer can have. I guess I thought that I loved him enough to be the one he settled for…until he actually asked me. At least he was honest and didn't try to wrap the proposal in romantic phrases."

"Are you sure he's still in love with her? He's been pretty upset that she kept Heather a secret from him."

"Oh, Dad, it's so obvious when you think about it. He was so upset the night she came here. Part of it was because of Heather, I know that. But I also think he was hurt when he heard she was getting married. He wouldn't admit that to me, of course. But I saw the pain in his eyes."

"Could be, I suppose. He doesn't talk about his feelings much."

"Tell me about it." She sat back in the chair and did her best to detach herself from the emotional turmoil she felt. "It's kind of interesting when you think about it. Every time I'm convinced that I've fully recovered from my passion for Jake, I end up being around him again. That's when I know that I'm not. Probably never will be. But that doesn't mean I have to make a decision that will end up making both of us miserable. A one-sided love would be miserable and I'm not willing to place myself in that position." She straightened and glanced at her watch. "I need to get a good night's sleep and deal with all of this tomorrow."

"You can stay here tonight, if you want."

She shook her head and stood up. He stood as well. "Thanks for the offer but all my things are at the house. Heather's nanny is supposed to be here tomorrow or Monday. I can hold out that long. Then I'll go home, lick my wounds and work to overcome my relapse."

Ken walked her to the door. He pulled her to him and

kissed her on the forehead. "You know, you could do a lot worse than to marry Jake. He'd be good to you, we both know that."

"I know. It's just that I can't marry someone who offers because he can't have the one he loves. I have more self-respect than that."

# Thirteen

**A**shley woke up the next morning relieved to discover that Jake had left and taken Heather with him. He'd left her a note in the kitchen, short and to the point.

*Heather and I will be gone most of the day.*

Which suited her just fine. The two of them had bonded and no longer needed her presence. She packed up her things, left her own brief note—"I've moved back home. Tell Heather I'll stay in touch."—and drove back to her apartment.

She'd done what she could for him and for his daughter. He'd found help, just what he'd told her he would do, and she was no longer needed. It wasn't his fault that she'd left her heart behind.

Now was the time to get over him and to get on with her life. She knew that would be a little tough since she intended to stay in touch with Heather. At least she wouldn't be seeing him. She'd make sure not to visit when he was there. That could be arranged easily enough. Because there was no way she'd step out of Heather's life. She'd already been abandoned once. Twice, if Ashley counted the loss of her great-grandmother. Ashley didn't want Heather to experience the pain she had gone through when her mother had abandoned her.

No. She would always be there for Heather.

Jake rented a car at the San Antonio airport and he and Heather went to meet Charlotte James.

"Why is she coming to live with us?"

"Because you need someone with you when you're not with me or Ashley."

"Oh."

Blessed silence…for almost ten seconds.

"Does she have kids like me?"

"Her name is Mrs. James. I'd appreciate it if you'd call her by her name."

"Mrs. James," she immediately parroted.

"That's right."

"Does Mrs. James have kids like me?"

"I don't think so. If she does, her children are probably grown."

"Is she old?"

"Uh," he stopped speaking because he needed to concentrate on the traffic. There was the exit sign for the street he was looking for. "Well," he said once they were off the freeway and stopped at a light, "I guess it depends on what you consider to be old."

"As old as you?"

Since he figured Mrs. James to be in her mid-fifties,

he wasn't certain how to answer that. Finally, he said, "Maybe she's little older than me. Why?"

"Will she get sick and will an am'blance come get her and take her away and I won't see her ever again?"

He glanced in the rearview mirror, where Heather sat in the car seat he'd brought with them. "You don't have to worry about that."

He hoped. Because if Mrs. James decided not to stay after the trial period, he would have to deal with Heather's fears.

Once they arrived at Charlotte's home and she met her, Heather seemed to relax. She was shy at first, as she usually was when she first met someone. Jake told Charlotte to enjoy the quiet while she could.

The three of them stopped at a kid-friendly restaurant for lunch and then took Heather to the zoo.

Jake had never seen Heather quite this excited before. After following Heather for more than an hour and listening to her running commentary, Charlotte smiled at Jake and said, "I see what you mean," and they both laughed.

Heather fell asleep in the plane. Once at the ranch, he held her while Charlotte installed the car seat, then put her down without her once stirring.

The zoo had worn her out. She wasn't the only one.

Heather woke up when they stopped in front of the house. "We're home!" she said gleefully.

She couldn't have said anything to make him feel happier. She'd adjusted to being left here with strangers remarkably well.

Heather said, "I gotta go tell Ashley what we did today!" at the same time that Jake realized her truck wasn't there.

"You may have to wait a little while because she's not here. Maybe she went to see her dad."

He moved Charlotte's luggage to the room where she'd be staying, which was close to Heather, so it was a while before he went downstairs for something to drink.

His note was still there, but something had been added. He read the note, then dropped it. So she was gone. Why did it hurt so much that she'd turned him down? She's just a kid, after all. She doesn't know what she wants.

Oh, really. And was that a kid in the shower and in bed with you?

His chest hurt. How could wanting to marry her because they'd slept together be insulting? Didn't he hear complaints from women he knew that most men were love 'em and leave 'em kind of guys?

Since he'd gotten to know Ashley as an adult, he'd been irritated with himself for marrying Tiffany. Why hadn't he waited until Ashley was an adult to marry a woman he was compatible with?

Too late to do that now. His past mistakes kept rearing their heads to haunt him. He'd have to learn to live with them. It wasn't the first time he'd been kicked in the face by a woman he loved. Or in Tiffany's case, thought he loved. Ashley's rejection hurt a thousand times more because he finally understood what love was all about and how deeply he'd been in love with Ashley as far back as her teenage years, if he'd just recognized it.

No wonder he'd reacted so violently to her sixteen-year-old kiss. Too bad he hadn't understood at the time what he was feeling. Somehow, he'd managed to screw up his life royally. At least he had Heather to love and care for. Having her would have to be enough.

"Hey, Jake, got a second?"

Jake had just come in from supervising the move of

a herd of sheep to a better feeding ground. There was nothing more stupid than sheep. If there was a wrong way to go, they would find it every time.

"Sure, Ken, what do you need?"

"Well, this is kind of personal, so I was wondering if you'd like to come over and have a cool one with me."

Jake glanced at his watch. "Sure. Heather won't be expecting me home for a while."

Ken slapped his back. "Good. See you at the house."

While Jake followed Ken's truck, he wondered what was wrong with Ken. Did he get some bad news about his health? Was something wrong with Ashley?

Don't go there. His breath became restricted every time he thought of her, just as though his lungs had stopped working.

When he walked into Ken's place, Ken was already standing there with a couple of bottles of cold beer. They drank in unison, wiped their mouths and grinned at each other before sprawling in Ken's comfortable chairs.

"Since Heather's been with me, I've switched to drinking iced tea at home, but I gotta tell ya, there's nothing like a cold beer on a hot Texas day!"

Ken smiled. "She's seemed settled in. How long has she been here?"

"Almost three weeks. She's got a birthday coming up soon. The folks promised to get back in time to plan one of their barbecue bashes for her."

"That's good. Really good. It'll be good to see Joe and Gail. They've been gone a while."

"They're the smart ones, you know. They like to spend summers in Washington and Oregon to get away from the heat. It will still be hot on the 28th of September, but they're willing to give up their comfort to meet their grandbaby."

"By the way," Ken said, "I meant to tell you that the sheriff called today. They found the car thieves on Mc-Grady's ranch, north of town. He thought you'd want to know."

"That's good to know."

They finished their beer and Ken went to get more. When he returned, Jake said, "You said there was something personal you wanted to talk to me about."

"Uh, yeah, that's right. It's probably none of my business but that's never stopped me before. Usually a dad asks a man if his intentions toward his daughter are honorable. In this case, I know yours are. I guess what I've been wondering is why you asked Ashley to marry you?"

Jake stared at him like the man had lost his mind. "Why the hell do you think, Ken?"

"Oh, I figure there could be several reasons. You need help with your daughter. You enjoy Ashley's company. You're tired of living alone."

"You seem to have as good an opinion of my character as Ashley. I thought you knew me better than that." He took another drink. "Just for the record, I asked her to marry me because I can't imagine my life without her in the center of it and because I'm crazy about her. Probably always have been, if you want to know the truth. I was just too dumb to understand what it was I was feeling all this time. Not that any of that matters. She turned me down."

"So I understand. Ashley's under the impression that you're still in love with Tiffany."

Jake shook his head in disbelief. "That's a bunch of crap and you know it as well as I do. I fell out of love with Tiffany years ago, if I ever loved her in the first place. I fell in love with who I thought she was. Once I got to know her, I learned my mistake. Ashley knows that."

"Does she? If you really love her, then you'd better

find a way to convince her of that. She's always worshipped you and, to be frank, I was hoping she'd outgrow it. For a while I thought she had...until your daughter showed up. That's when I knew Ashley had only been kidding me as well as herself that she'd gotten over her feelings for you."

Jake squeezed his eyes closed. "Tiffany is part of the past I can't change. The only good thing that happened from the marriage was Heather. I want to look forward to the future instead of spending energy dwelling on past mistakes that can't be undone."

"I know you were pretty torn up when she left you."

"I don't deny that, but it wasn't because I loved her. I was shocked at her leaving so unexpectedly. I didn't have a clue that she was making plans to divorce me. I really thought I'd done everything possible to make the marriage work."

"From what I could see, you did."

"It was the sense of failure that continued to eat at me long after I accepted that she was gone."

Ken smiled ruefully. "You know, Jake, you couldn't have chosen to marry two women more opposite from each other."

Jake nodded. "I know. I'd like to think I'm older and wiser now, Ken. But Ashley's made it clear she doesn't want to marry me and I have to respect her decisions. She deserves to be loved and cherished. I hope she finds the man who will do that."

"Ever thought about explaining your feelings to her?"

"You mean, tell her she's out of her mind if she thinks I have any feelings for Tiffany?"

"Well, maybe you might want to do it without calling her crazy. Just a suggestion, of course. I'm a little curious. Did you happen to mention that you're in love with her and have been for years?"

"Of course I did! It didn't seem to matter to her, though." Jake rubbed the cold bottle across his forehead. "I don't know, Ken. I think she mentioned Tiffany to you as an excuse. I used to believe that she truly loved me, but hell, I don't know anything anymore. All I know is she turned me down and moved out. Pretty strong evidence that she meant what she said."

# Fourteen

**A** week after she left the ranch, Ashley arrived home in time to hear her phone ringing. Good grief. Couldn't she at least get inside before her phone started to ring off the wall? Obviously not.

"All right!" she said after the fourth ring. "I'm coming, I'm coming." She grabbed the phone and took a deep breath. "H'lo?"

"Hi, sweetheart. Haven't heard from you in a while. How's life treatin' you?"

"Hi, Dad. How've you been?"

"Good. And you?"

"Very well, actually. Our new vet started with us last week and he's already carrying his load. Woody and I are finally getting out earlier because of the extra help."

"Ah, that explains it. When I called the office, Wendy said you'd already left."

"So what's up?" She was tired and at the moment just wanted to take a cool shower and relax.

"The reason I'm calling," Ken said, "is to invite my favorite girl to go out to dinner with me tonight. Are you up for it?"

She glanced at her watch. "What a nice idea. I'd love to have dinner with you. Dress or casual?"

"You have to ask?"

She laughed. "Okay. Jeans it is."

"I'm leaving now."

"I'll be here."

She was in the shower when she realized that Heather's birthday was coming up in a couple of weeks. She needed to talk to Jake to see what he wanted to do about the party he'd mentioned having for Heather. Her heart did a double beat at the thought of seeing him again…as a friend only.

She spoke to Heather on the phone almost every day. A couple of times, Charlotte had brought her in to the clinic to say hi when they were in town. Charlotte was a jewel and Heather adored her. She was glad to see that the feeling was mutual.

She hadn't seen Jake since she'd moved back in town. That wasn't really surprising, since she'd seen next to nothing of him before he called her that one memorable night.

She shook her head as she toweled off and started dressing. Was she sorry for answering his distress call that night?

She didn't have an answer. She understood the adult Jake much better now that she was an adult. Unfortunately for her, her newfound knowledge had only made her love him more.

Heather had brought out mothering instincts Ashley would never have believed she was capable of feeling.

After all, she was her mother's child and her mother had made it clear when she left that she wasn't cut out for raising a kid and taking care of a husband. So maybe Ashley wasn't like her mother, after all.

How could she be sorry for learning more about herself and Jake?

The knowledge, however, didn't take the pain of loss away.

Ken took her to one of the steak houses on the outskirts of town. She liked the rustic atmosphere and friendly waitresses. After they ordered and their drinks arrived, Ken said, "You're looking good, kiddo."

"Thank you, Dad. You, on the other hand, are pushing yourself too hard."

He shrugged. "I'm no spring chicken, but I do a full day's work without complaining."

"To what do I owe this honor—you driving into town after a long day? Anything special?"

He took a drink from his large glass of iced tea. "Well, I guess there is, although I know I should come in more often to see you. Time just slips by so quick, you know?"

She reached over and patted his hand. "I know, Dad."

He cleared his throat. "The thing is, I, uh, spoke to Jake this afternoon."

Since she knew that Jake and her dad spoke every day, his nervousness must mean that they'd discussed her.

"Oh?"

"He's hurtin', Ashley. He's hurtin' real bad."

Fear shot through her. Jake had been hurt? When? How? "Oh, no! What happened? Was he in an accident? Why didn't somebody tell me? I talked to Heather yesterday and she never—"

"He's been having some trouble gettin' around ever since you ripped his heart right out of his chest."

She leaned back in her chair. "What are you talking about, Dad? I haven't done anything to Jake."

"You refused to marry him."

"I never knew you had such a flare for drama. Ripped his heart out, indeed. What nonsense. He was probably relieved, actually. You know Jake. Always doing the right thing."

"Why would him proposing be doing the right thing? Or do I want to know?"

"You don't want to know."

"Damn." He sat there silently drinking his tea. Neither one of them spoke until after their steaks were delivered.

As far as Ashley concerned, the subject was over.

Halfway through their meal, Ken said, "Is there a possibility that just maybe he had others reasons to want to marry you?"

"Are we still talking about Jake?" she asked whimsically, picking up her glass.

"You mean you've got other men proposing to you?"

"I was teasing, Dad. Do you think you know those reasons?"

"You know what your problem is, missy," he said, pointing his fork at her. "You think too much like a woman!"

She laughed. "Imagine that."

"Jake doesn't wear his feelings on his sleeve. Never has. Doesn't mean he doesn't have 'em. He's so blamed in love with you, he's plain pitiful."

"Did he tell you that?"

"As a matter of fact, he did. He also told me that not only did he not love Tiffany, he didn't even like her. Once he got a good look at the woman he married and how little they had in common, he realized that marrying her was the biggest mistake he ever made." He paused. "You know good and well that that man dotes on you. Always has."

"When I was a child, Dad."

"Well, for your information, his feelings have gotten even worse…I mean, even stronger, ever since you stayed out there with him and Heather. You 'bout broke his heart when you refused to marry him."

She stared at her dad in dismay. Could she have made the biggest mistake of her life when she told Jake she wouldn't marry him?

He was in love with her? Well, he'd said so, but in such a casual way she figured he loved her like he loved Blue Bell ice cream.

"Men!" she finally muttered. "It wouldn't have hurt for him to tell me the reason he wanted to marry me was that he was in love with me, instead of all that stuff about Heather needing a mother figure and because I loved *him*!"

"Have you ever known Jake to be real open about how he felt about things?"

The only time he'd opened up to her was the night after Heather arrived. He'd shared his vulnerability with her. Would he have done that with someone he didn't trust and love?

Knowing Jake as well as she did, she had to admit that, no, he generally kept his feelings to himself.

She looked at Ken, feeling awful that she hadn't understood all of this before now. "What do you think I should do?"

"How should I know? I just wanted you to look at things from his viewpoint. I don't know how to get you to fix things with him."

After Ashley went to bed that night, she couldn't stop herself from going over and over her conversation with her dad.

Jake loved her. Why was that so hard to believe? She'd allowed her fear that he would never love her in the way he'd loved Tiffany to blind her to what was happening between them.

He loved her too much to take advantage of their situation.

He loved her enough to propose to her after making it clear to everyone in the county that he never intended to marry again.

He loved her.

She groaned.

She had to talk to him.

She had to apologize to him.

She had to get down on her knees and beg his forgiveness—the sooner the better.

She would go out to the ranch tomorrow after work. She needed to see Heather anyway and she'd enjoy visiting with Charlotte again. Somehow she had to make him understand how much she loved him and how much she wanted to marry him.

And pray that it wasn't too late to make amends.

# Fifteen

**H**eather was the first person to greet Ashley when she arrived at the ranch the next afternoon.

"You came, you came! Yea! Guess what? Me and Miss Charlotte are making gingerbread men! Wanna help?"

"Sounds like fun." Heather grabbed her hand and pulled her along to the kitchen. "Miss Charlotte. Look who's here. Ashley!"

"Hi, Charlotte," Ashley said, sounding breathless.

Charlotte James was comfortably middle-aged, with a calm demeanor and a sweet smile. No wonder Heather liked her. Charlotte looked and acted like a loving grandmother.

"I want you to know that you've won top marks with Heather," Ashley said. "She told me on the phone yesterday that your allowing her to splash in the tub makes you wonderful."

Charlotte laughed. Her laugh was contagious and Ashley joined her. Jake had found a gem in Charlotte.

"How do you like living in the Hill Country?" Ashley asked.

"Oh, I was raised in this area, not far from Fredericksburg. Hal's job took us to San Antonio years ago. After he died, I wanted to come back to this area to live. This job seemed the answer to my prayers."

"Do you have children?"

"Yes. Two boys and a girl…all grown…and none of them interested in making me a grandmother. I consider Heather to be a true blessing in my life. She makes me feel young again."

"I'm glad. She's really special."

"I am?" Heather asked.

"That you are."

"Oh. What does special mean?"

The women laughed. "That I love you very much," Ashley replied.

"That's good." She went back to working on her gingerbread man. Ashley could spot the ones Heather had made because they each struck a different pose. One thing that could be said about Heather—she was certainly creative.

Later, after being an eyewitness to the amount of water Heather could splash on the floor, Ashley said, "I expected that Jake would be home by now."

"He said he goes to town on Fridays and for us not to wait up for him."

Ashley hit her forehead with the palm of her hand. "Of course he does! I can't believe I forgot what day it is. Since I really need to talk to him, I think I'll wait up for him. It would be fun to spend the rest of the evening with Heather." She didn't want to put off her meeting with Jake one more day.

\* \* \*

Jake pulled up beside Ashley's truck sometime after midnight. He wasn't happy to see it sitting there. If she followed Tiffany's example, she was probably waiting inside to offer him his child. Of course, that wouldn't work too well, considering the fact that they'd been together one night and—

Oh, sh—! That could be *exactly* why she was here…to tell him that she was pregnant. Could she tell this soon? He wasn't up on all that stuff. Had she decided to marry him after all?

He sighed.

Heather would be over the moon if she agreed to marry him.

As for him, he'd discovered what his life was like without Ashley.

Lonely.

Sad.

Make that heartbroken.

He opened the door of his truck.

Jake walked into the house with measured steps, pausing only long enough to figure out where she was.

Ah, there she was, asleep on the sofa in the living room.

He sat across from her, looking for any changes since he'd last seen her. She still looked too fragile for comfort. She'd lost weight. Maybe. If he were to strip off her clothing, he would know for sure.

Still wanting her in your bed, Crenshaw? Of course he was. He wanted her next to him for the next fifty years or so, the first person he saw each and every morning of his life.

Ashley stirred and looked at her wristwatch. She sat up and only then did she see him.

She blinked in surprise. "I didn't hear you come in."

"Mm."

"Have you been here long?"

"Ashley, you aren't here at this time of night in order to make polite conversation. Just say what you came to say."

"Oh." She frowned. "Well, I was hoping you'd be in a better mood."

"I'm not."

"You know, I kind of figured that out for myself." She looked at him as though waiting for him to say something.

He looked at his watch meaningfully. He hoped she'd get the message. The last thing he wanted was to see her when he felt so vulnerable.

She let out a whoosh of air. "All right, then." She gave him a timid smile. "You're probably wondering why I called this meeting." When he didn't change expression, she gave a tiny shrug. "Trying for a little humor here." She glanced down at her clasped hands and then brought her gaze to meet his. "First of all, I owe you a big apology. Once I realized that, I didn't want to wait another day to tell you."

He continued to wait for the purpose of this visit.

"I misunderstood the purpose of your proposal."

He raised his brows. "Really. Seemed clear enough to me at the time."

She rubbed her eyes. "I'm not saying this well." The silence that followed gave Jake the opportunity to feast his eyes on her—damn, but he loved this woman! He was already as hard as a rock and there wasn't a thing he could do about it. Did she have any idea how much her rejection hurt him? Did she think an apology would make it better?

She cleared her throat. "I had dinner with Dad last night. He said I had hurt your feel—actually, he put it more dramatically, but the gist of his conversation was that I'd hurt you."

He shrugged. "I'll get over it."

He told me that you were in love with me."

"I told you the same thing."

"I didn't hear it in the same way, then. You also talked about your guilt for making love to me—before the wedding. You talked about my relationship with Heather and I thought you wanted to marry me because it would be convenient."

"Convenient!" Jake jumped up and glowered at her, his hands on his hips. "You are the least convenient woman I've ever known in my life! You drive me crazy and have for years. Convenience had nothing to do with my asking you to marry me!"

He reminded himself not to call her an idiot, but he came very close at that moment. He took a deep breath. "I've loved you all your life. I thought I made that clear to you a long time ago. I've been in love with you since you were sixteen, when I was ashamed to have such lustful thoughts about a teenager. I thought you were too young for me. After the divorce, I knew I'd blown my chance with you, but not ever during that time have I not been in love with you. So yeah, I guess you could say that my feelings were hurt when you turned me down. But that's life and I'm dealing with it."

He spun around and went over to the window in an effort to cool off before he said too much. What would that be, anyway? He'd just poured out his soul to her. What more did she want. Blood?

When she spoke she was directly behind him, causing his muscles to contract.

"Is there any way you can forgive me for being a complete idiot?"

Guess it was okay if she called herself that, as long as he didn't. He slowly turned and looked at her. "Ashley, just tell me what it is you want from me, okay? I guess I'm too dense to understand why you're here."

She folded her arms. "Because I want to marry you," she said quietly.

He never knew what to expect from her. Tonight was no different.

"Don't tease me, Ashley. You've already got me at the end of my rope."

She dropped her arms and walked closer. She placed her hands on his chest and said, "I do well and truly love you, Jake Crenshaw. I loved you as a child, as a teenager and as an adult. I can't imagine marrying anyone but you, if you still want me."

"That's never been the question." The truth began to seep into his brain. She loved him and she wanted to marry him. He prayed he wasn't dreaming. He pulled her against him and held her, his heart beating wildly. This was really happening. "I want to marry you, too," he mumbled hoarsely, not certain she could tell what he'd said around the lump in his throat.

She held on to him with a tight grip, her arms encircling his waist. He felt her trembling as he leaned his head on top of hers.

"I love you so much that I ache inside," he whispered. "I don't know how else to tell you so that you'll believe me."

"I believe you. I want to marry you as soon as possible, especially if you don't intend to make love to me until after the wedding."

He laughed out loud, swinging her around in a circle. "I believe we can work something out about that. I suggest we go upstairs and discuss the matter."

He looked down at her and saw tears in her eyes. "I'd like that," she whispered.

Jake picked her up and carried her to his room.

As soon as he closed the bedroom door behind them, Jake carried her into the bathroom and placed her on her feet. He reached into the shower and turned on the water.

"I think we need to start our shower over, don't you? As I recall, we were forced to end it a little prematurely." He was teasing her again, like he always used to do. Ashley felt like laughing and crying at the same time. What if her dad hadn't talked to her? She would never have known how wrong she'd been about him.

It didn't bear thinking about.

He took his time undressing first her, then him. After adjusting the spray, he stepped under the water and tugged her in as well.

This really was like that afternoon, only this time she knew darned well she wasn't dreaming.

He took the soap and, filling his hands with lather, caressed her body, leaving trails of bubbles to mark his path. Her knees were trembling so much she wasn't sure they were going to hold.

She leaned against the tile, much as he had done that first time, and let him explore every inch of her body. Until now, she'd not known she had so many erogenous zones—the backs of her knees, the arch of her foot, her ears, her neck, her—

She stopped thinking.

By the time they were out of the shower and he was drying her off, she wanted him so badly that she was shaking. He quickly ran the towel over himself, took her hand and led her to the bed.

Once they were lying side by side, he raised up on his elbow, resting his head on his hand. "Now let's see," he drawled, "I believe we were going to discuss dates for our wedding—" She stopped him with a kiss.

He already had her teetering on the edge and if she couldn't see the evidence with her own eyes, she would think that the only thing on his mind at the moment was to have a lazy discussion.

"Yes, I believe that was the subject we were discussing downstairs," she finally replied, inches from his mouth. She slid her hand from his chest down to his groin, wrapping her fingers around that very evidence. He jolted up like a jackknife, pushing her hand away.

"No fair. You're going to have this over with before we've started."

"Really? And what was that you were doing to me in the shower?"

He grinned. "My, you really do have a memory problem. Here. Let me show you."

He leaned over her and wrapped his moist tongue around the tip of her breast while his hands moved over her. He began to kiss her, starting with the arch of her foot and not stopping until he was stretched out over her, his mouth locked with hers.

Once again, his magic fingers touched her wetness and he slowly stroked her until she lifted her hips toward him, mutely pleading for him to take her.

As though he could no longer ignore her invitation, he slid deeply inside her, rocking gently against her.

"I love you so much," she whispered into his ear and he turned his head to catch her lips with his, never slowing down. His pace quickened until they were both panting. She wrapped her legs and arms around him, pushing to be as close to him as she could get until each of them was straining to envelop the other.

Ashley cried out when her body seemed to explode into a million pieces of joy. His groan immediately followed as he continued to move rapidly within her, eventually collapsing on top of her.

His harsh breathing caused the wisps of hair around

her ear to flutter and she realized that she was breathing just as rapidly.

Ashley felt lazily content and was drifting toward sleep when he began to kiss her once again. She felt him hard against her thigh and reached for him, guiding him inside.

She felt that they were making love in slow motion, each movement choreographed to excite the other. She nipped the lobe of his ear and then licked it, causing him to shudder. He palmed her breast and massaged it until she knew she couldn't take much more.

She grabbed his butt and pushed him into a faster rhythm, meeting him thrust after thrust, and making him laugh.

She loved to hear Jake laugh. It made her want to laugh with joy, as well.

This time when they broke through the pleasure barrier, he rolled to her side. He lay there, face down, without moving.

"Jake?" she whispered. "Are you all right?"

"Mmph."

"Oh. Well, I feel much better now. Thanks for the reassurance."

He turned his head to see her. "You know, I don't remember your having such a smart mouth."

"I learn from my elders," she replied primly.

He chuckled without moving.

Eventually Jake went into the bathroom. When he returned to bed, he drew her head onto his shoulder. "You know, when I saw your truck parked in front of the house, I thought you might be here to tell me you're pregnant."

She didn't say anything.

He gave her a little shake. "So. Are you pregnant?"

She smiled at him and said, "Not yet, cowboy, but at the rate we're going, it's only a matter of time."

# Epilogue

The Crenshaws were having a barbecue and everyone for miles around had been invited.

Joe and Gail Crenshaw were back from their latest trip.

Jared had flown in from Saudi Arabia.

Jude drove in from his undercover assignment in San Antonio.

Only Jason wasn't there. He had made the Army a career and worked in special ops, so there were several hot spots in the world where he might be. No one really knew where he was or how to contact him. Gail sent regular e-mails to him and he responded when he could without telling her where he was.

However, there were enough cousins, aunts and uncles there to make up for his absence.

Strings of lights were in all the trees. There were live musicians, lots to eat, plenty to drink, a great deal of talk and a great deal of laughter.

Everyone had gathered in order to officially meet Jake's four-year-old daughter on her birthday. The large group must have intimidated her because she'd been clinging to Jake, who was carrying her, since people had begun to appear.

"Honey, don't you want to get down and go play with Mary Ann?" he asked her. "See?" he pointed. "She's over there with her mother."

"Uh-uh." She tightened the deathlike grip she had on his neck.

"Uh, then could you ease your hold on me a little so I can breathe?"

There might have been a slight lessening of her hold. Very slight.

"I thought you'd enjoy having a birthday party, sweetheart. You're finally four years old today. You were so excited while we were planning this party. You helped blow up balloons and decorate your pretty cake. We're supposed to be celebrating, you know. Don't be scared."

She buried her head in his shoulder.

"You have to admit, Jake," Ashley said at his side, "seeing so many Crenshaws gathered in one place can be a little daunting. She'll get used to them soon enough. Just give her some time and she'll adjust."

"Well, I need to go help Dad—"

"You're doing exactly what you're supposed to be doing, you know...being Heather's safe place. Your dad's been doing this for years. I doubt he needs any assistance."

He kissed the top of Heather's curls. "So," he said, peering down at her, "you're going to spend the evening in my arms, is that it?"

She nodded her head and Jake laughed.

"What's so funny?" Jared asked, sauntering up to them, holding a drink in his hand.

"I'm just enjoying my daughter. How are things with you?"

"Let's just say I'm glad to be home after the past fourteen months overseas."

"It was pretty bad over there, huh?"

"Worse than bad but I managed to survive. I don't have to go back until the first of the year." He turned to Ashley. "It's good seeing you here with Jake, Ashley. The three of you look like a family."

Jake cocked his head. "You know, that's an idea." He turned to Ashley. "What do you think, honey? Jared may have a good idea there." Ashley punched his free arm, then held out her left hand to show Jared her engagement ring.

"Wow! When did *this* happen?"

Ashley thought a moment before she said, "Oh, somewhere around my seventh birthday. It just took Jake a while to give me the ring."

Jared laughed. "Good point, Ashley. I'm glad everything has worked out for y'all. I'm serious; Jake, I've never seen you so happy."

"That's not surprising since I've never been this happy before."

Heather raised her head. "Daddy?"

"What, sweetheart."

"'Member when you said I could have a puppy?"

Jake's eyes widened in dismay. He looked at Ashley, silently pleading for help. She returned his gaze with a smile, her raised eyebrow signaling he was on his own with this one.

He cleared his throat. "Well, yes. Yes, I do. It's just that—"

"Can I get my puppy tonight?"

"May I?" Ashley asked.

He lowered his brow in a mock frown. "Not you, too."

Heather knew what she meant. "*May* I have my puppy tonight?" She grinned at him. "It's for my birthday."

If she but knew it, he'd walk barefoot over hot coals for this little girl. However, that didn't mean she could have everything she wanted. Besides, after the night he'd first mentioned the idea, she'd never said another word about wanting a puppy until now.

"Don't you want to wait a while to get a puppy?" he asked hopefully. "Puppies take lots of care and training."

She shook her head, her eyes sad.

Jake looked at Jared and Ashley and sighed. "If you'll excuse us. It looks like we have to go see a man about a dog."

Jared watched him walk away before he turned to Ashley. "I don't know what you did, Ashley, but you somehow made a new man out of Jake. None of us ever expected him to get married again. How did you do it?"

"I just loved him, Jared, like I always have. I guess he finally got around to noticing."

Jared laughed. "Don't kid yourself. I remember one of your birthday parties when he couldn't keep his eyes off you. Do you remember that?"

"One of my fondest memories. Why?"

"I knew then that he was in conflict with himself over you. I'm glad he finally resolved it satisfactorily."

"Me, too."

Jared looked around them before quietly asking, "Has Tiffany contacted him since the night she brought Heather to him?"

Ashley shook her head no. "He had his attorney draw up papers for her to sign giving up all her rights to Heather. I believe they're waiting for her to return from some long trip to sign them."

"Hard to imagine not wanting your own kid."

"How about you? When are you planning to get married and settle down?"

"Me?" He laughed. "You got the wrong guy for that one. I love the ladies but I never met one I wanted to face over the breakfast table every morning for the rest of my life. No, marriage is fine for y'all. I enjoy my freedom too much."

Gail came over to join them. "I think everyone's enjoying themselves tonight, don't you?" she asked.

Jared draped his arm across his mother's shoulders. "What's not to enjoy, Mom? You know how people look forward to your parties. Always have, always will."

"That's good to know," she said. Looking at Ashley, she added, "While I've got you here, I want to talk to you about planning an engagement party for you and Jake soon."

Jared groaned. "Hey, planning engagement parties creeps me out. I'll see y'all later." He waved and walked away.

Gail watched him saunter away and said, "You know what's going to happen to that young man one of these days, don't you? He going to meet a woman who'll have him so tied up in knots he won't know which way to turn. He'll be begging her to marry him, mark my words."

"Couldn't happen to a more deserving guy, if you ask me."

They both laughed.

"Isn't Heather adorable?" Gail asked Ashley a few minutes later, nodding toward Jake, who now held his daughter in one arm and a wriggling black-and-white puppy in the other.

"Absolutely," Ashley replied, watching Heather try to pet the puppy without letting go of Jake's neck.

"You don't suppose we're prejudiced, do you? Because she's ours?"

"Absolutely not. Anyone can see that we're merely stating facts."

Gail grinned at her response. "It's so much fun to watch Jake with her, isn't it? He's adapted to fatherhood rather quickly, considering the circumstances."

Ashley smiled. "Yes, but I'm not surprised, really. Remember how he was with me when I was a child?"

"Yes, of course. He was always so proud of you, just as if you belonged to him."

"I do, Gail. I belong to Jake. Always have…always will."

* * * * *

*We hope you enjoyed BRANDED,*
*the first book in Annette Broadrick's*
*new Desire series,* THE CRENSHAWS *of Texas.*

*Please look for the story of Jake's brother,*
*Jared—back from the oil fields of Saudi Arabia—*
*and Lindsay—elegant and off-limits—*
*who found themselves*
*CAUGHT IN THE CROSSFIRE*
*of a manipulative and ruthless power broker,*
*in the second book of the Crenshaw series*
*(Desire 1610) next month.*

*For a sneak preview of*
*CAUGHT IN THE CROSSFIRE, turn the page...*

# One

Jared abruptly came awake at the sound of a crashing door. At that moment, he was aware of only two things—he had the mother of all hangovers and the door to his bedroom had flown open hard enough to bounce off the wall.

Since he lived alone, there was no reason for anyone to come charging into the room.

He painfully squinted his eyes open and discovered that the pounding in his head was the least of his problems.

This wasn't his bedroom. So where the hell was he? He stared at the lace-edged canopy above him before slowly moving his gaze to the rest of the room. His bedroom sure as hell didn't smell like flowers or contain this delicate furniture.

He stared at a wall of shelves filled with fancy-dressed dolls before he closed his eyes again.

Maybe the hangover was affecting his vision. He softly massaged his eyes. When he opened them again, he stared in shock.

Two men stood just inside the doorway.

He was having a nightmare, that's what it was. Either that or he'd died and gone straight to hell. He could think of no other reason why his father would be standing in the room with Senator Russell.

Lindsey Russell's father.

What the—?

Jared turned his head and then grabbed it before it tumbled off his shoulders. Lindsey Russell lay on the pillow beside him, facing him, her hand tucked beneath her cheek. How she could still be asleep after the racket the men had made was beyond him.

In fact, everything was beyond him at the moment.

What was he doing in bed with her?

He knew what their visitors thought…hell, he'd be thinking the same thing given their circumstances. What he couldn't figure out was what he was doing here. Even more important, why had she allowed him into her bed?

They'd been seeing each other, sure, but he'd known from the very beginning of their relationship that she wouldn't sleep with him.

He liked her. He liked her a lot. If she'd given him any sign that she would take the next step, he would have been all for it. Is that what happened last night?

If so, why couldn't he remember?

How had he gotten here? He forced himself to think back to the night before.

He hadn't done anything in particular, as he recalled. After hard physical labor all day working for
Jake on the ranch, he'd cleaned up at his place and
driven into town for something to eat. He'd run into a
couple of guys he knew at the Mustang Bar & Grill,
so after he ate, he'd stayed a while and shot some pool
with them.

He hadn't been drinking. Well, maybe a couple of
beers, but nothing that would cause him to wake up
with a pounding headache and no idea how he ended up
in Lindsay's bed.

He stared at the men who stood in silence looking at
him as though he were pond scum.

He really couldn't blame them. If there was one
thing that Jared knew on this particular morning, it
was that he had no business being in Lindsey Russell's bed.

What had he been thinking?

Jared pushed himself up, rested his elbows on his
bent knees and held his head. "I can explain —" he said
slowly, his voice the sound of a croaking bullfrog. He
cleared his throat. "You see," he said and then paused.
He looked at his dad, who now leaned against the doorjamb with his arms crossed and one booted foot across
the other. Next, he glanced at Lindsey who had stirred
at the sound of his voice. "Actually," he continued, "I
have no idea how I got here or why I'm here."

His gaze kept going back to Lindsey, who looked
amazingly pretty first thing in the morning, her face
slightly flushed with sleep, and her dark hair tumbled
around her shoulders and draped across her pillow.

He forced his gaze back to the men.

Joe lifted an eyebrow. "Oh, I think R.W. and I can figure out that last one without any explanation on your part," Joe drawled softly.

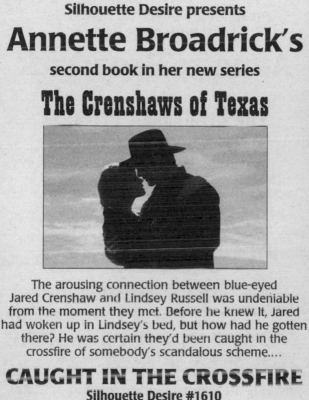

# Silhouette

# Desire

**Presenting a powerful new series
from bestselling author**

# Annette Broadrick

## The Crenshaws of Texas

Hell-raisers, adventurers and risk takers,
the Crenshaw men run a ranch the size of
Rhode Island, wrest oil from the ground in
some of the most dangerous places in the world
and fight to the death for their country.

**Read the stories of two of these
rugged Texans and the spirited women
who bring them to their knees in**

# BRANDED
**(Silhouette Desire #1604, on sale September 2004)**

# CAUGHT IN THE CROSSFIRE
**(Silhouette Desire #1610, on sale October 2004)**

**And look for the rest of the Crenshaws in 2005.**

*Available at your favorite retail outlet.*

If you enjoyed what you just read,
then we've got an offer you can't resist!

# Take 2 bestselling
# love stories FREE!

# Plus get a FREE surprise gift!

---

**Clip this page and mail it to Silhouette Reader Service™**

**IN U.S.A.**
3010 Walden Ave.
P.O. Box 1867
Buffalo, N.Y. 14240-1867

**IN CANADA**
P.O. Box 609
Fort Erie, Ontario
L2A 5X3

**YES!** Please send me 2 free Silhouette Desire® novels and my free surprise gift. After receiving them, if I don't wish to receive anymore, I can return the shipping statement marked cancel. If I don't cancel, I will receive 6 brand-new novels every month, before they're available in stores! In the U.S.A., bill me at the bargain price of $3.80 plus 25¢ shipping and handling per book and applicable sales tax, if any*. In Canada, bill me at the bargain price of $4.47 plus 25¢ shipping and handling per book and applicable taxes**. That's the complete price and a savings of at least 10% off the cover prices—what a great deal! I understand that accepting the 2 free books and gift places me under no obligation ever to buy any books. I can always return a shipment and cancel at any time. Even if I never buy another book from Silhouette, the 2 free books and gift are mine to keep forever.

225 SDN DZ9F
326 SDN DZ9G

| | | |
|---|---|---|
| Name | (PLEASE PRINT) | |
| Address | Apt.# | |
| City | State/Prov. | Zip/Postal Code |

*Not valid to current Silhouette Desire® subscribers.*

*Want to try two free books from another series?*
*Call 1-800-873-8635 or visit www.morefreebooks.com.*

\* Terms and prices subject to change without notice. Sales tax applicable in N.Y.
\*\* Canadian residents will be charged applicable provincial taxes and GST.
All orders subject to approval. Offer limited to one per household.
® are registered trademarks owned and used by the trademark owner and or its licensee.

DES04R                                      ©2004 Harlequin Enterprises Limited